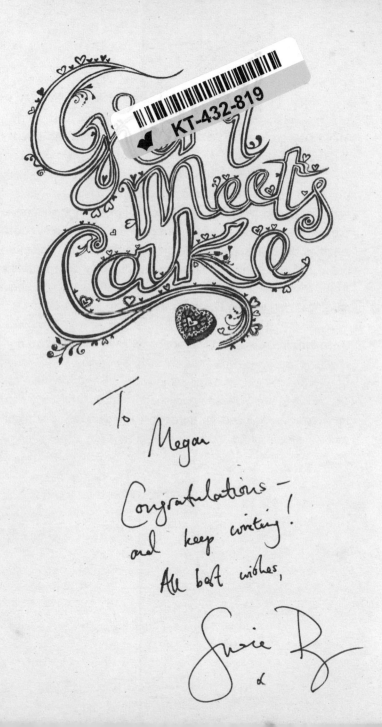

To Megan

Congratulations —
and keep writing!
All best wishes,

Susie B
x

Susie Day grew up in Penarth, Wales, with a lisp and a really unfortunate first name.

Her many careers have included guiding tourists, professional nappy-changing, teaching small people how many beans make five and taller people how to interrogate the beans from a post-structuralist perspective, and herding boarding school students – but she always wanted to be a writer. She firmly believes in the dictum "write what you know", which is why this book is about cake, watching telly, and helpless romantic flailitude.

Susie lives in Oxford, and is probably drinking a cup of tea right now (she usually has one around this time of day).

Her novel, BIG WOO!, was published in 2008: "I honestly don't think I've *ever* laughed so hard while reading . . . very highly recommended" *Chicklish*.

Girl Meets Cake

Susie Day

MARION LLOYD BOOKS

First published in the UK in 2009 by Marion Lloyd Books
An imprint of Scholastic Ltd
Euston House, 24 Eversholt Street
London, NW1 1DB, UK
Registered office: Westfield Road, Southam, Warwickshire, CV47 0RA
SCHOLASTIC and associated logos are trademarks
and/or registered trademarks of Scholastic Inc.

ISBN 978 1 407 10938 1

A CIP catalogue record for this book is
available from the British Library

Printed in the UK by CPI Bookmarque, Croydon, CR0 4TD
Papers used by Scholastic Children's Books are
made from wood grown in sustainable forests.

1 3 5 7 9 10 8 6 4 2

This is a work of fiction. Names, characters, places,
incidents and dialogues are products of the author's imagination
or are used fictitiously. Any resemblance to actual people, living
or dead, events or locales is entirely coincidental.

www.scholastic.co.uk/zone

for Tina, absurdly brilliant sister and locator of the carrot cake

Recipe for a Heidi

Ingredients:

Hair (plaited)
2 eyes (brown)
Assorted other body parts
Epic DVD collection
Detective skills
Tendency to fall in love with imaginary people

Method:

- Whisk all ingredients with parental implements until thoroughly mixed up
- Dump resulting goop (including parental implements) in the Goldfinch School for Troublemaking Drop-Out Freaks
- Bake until mental

"Poop on a fork, Heidi. What part of 'I don't want to see your face in here Saturday' did you not follow?" Betsy yells before I'm even halfway through the door of the Little Leaf cafe.

Which is OK, because she owns the place. And is my second-favourite human being in the universe. And anyway she's American, so the whole Traditional British Hospitality thing is allowed to pass her by.

She tries though. If you don't look too closely, the Little Leaf is a perfect picture-postcard tearoom on the village green. It sells home-made scones with jam and clotted cream, twenty-four different kinds of tea and only one kind of coffee (instant and horrible), and there are lacy tablecloths on half of the tables. There's even a shelf running round the ceiling displaying novelty teapots in the shape of red London buses.

But then you notice the walls: tangerine, sky blue and pink – one of each, with a dusty black wall behind the counter, which Betsy uses as a chalkboard for the day's specials, and the Daily Wisdom: SMILE! *it makes me remember to wash my hands before serving you.* EAT A CAKE! *or the kitten dies.* There are squashy sofas and armchairs infiltrating their way between the lace tablecloths. The shelf with the buses also has dragons, a bust of Shakespeare with a red plastic clown nose, and a selection of novelty hats, from deerstalker to top. There's even a picture of the Queen (and you can only see the felt-pen moustache if you stand on a chair).

Tourists eat it up. Tourists take photos of themselves pointing at the menu. Locals go to the Big Bean coffee house opposite for venti mochas.

I still smile every time I walk through the door anyway, even after spending all summer in a Little Leaf frilly apron, juggling teapots and getting raspberry jam smeared up to my elbows. You get free cake when you're a waitress. Sometimes even on your day off.

I hope.

A few heads turn as I sidle past: two cardiganish old ladies from the town (cream tea x 2); a couple of guys in the corner in bright-red anoraks and hiking boots, maps and guide books all over the table (Earl Grey, almond slice, angel cake). Pretty quiet for a Saturday afternoon – but it's September, end of season. Back to school time for the tourists too.

"Very welcoming, ta," I say, bagging myself a stool at the counter.

"Sincerely, honeybee, it's always a pleasure," says Betsy, setting me up with a pot of Assam tea without me needing to ask, sliding fistfuls of jangly bangles up her arms. "But aren't you supposed to be a little occupied right now? You know, studying, or whatever it is you kids do up there on the hill?"

It's arrivals day. The day they open up the posh Manor entrance, with its big stone pillars and big stone steps, and welcome the Finches back to the nest. The Goldfinch is where you get sent when you've been kicked out of everywhere else – if your parents can afford it. Today's the day all the Finchy freaks promise Mumsy and Papa they won't get expelled again this year, and wave goodbye to parents till Christmas, as the chauffeurs in the shiny cars wheelspin on the gravel and speed down the drive to safety.

"Nobody's back yet," I tell her.

Nobody I want to see anyway. Tho Mothership dragged me up there last week to help her count the hockey sticks in the PE stores, ready for the new term, and I sneaked away to check the arrivals schedule in Dad Man's little office. Fili and Ludo are due at 4p.m. Dai's flight gets in at 6, assuming he manages not to miss it this time. These facts may just possibly be written on my calendar, and in my phone, and on the back of my hand in red felt pen, just in case.

"Anyway, I can't stay away. I think I may be addicted to your carrot cake."

"That'll be the teaspoonful of crack cocaine in every slice," comes Teddy's voice from the kitchen out the back.

Betsy rolls her eyes, scrubs out today's Wisdom (NO, WE DON'T DO CAPPUCCINO! *or any other monk-based beverages*), and replaces it with OUR CARROT CAKE DOES NOT CONTAIN ILLEGAL NARCOTICS.

Teddy ducks out of the kitchen, adds "*Today*" underneath, grins and sneaks back out of sight.

Teddy is Betsy's seventeen-year-old son, and the Little Leaf's other addictive ingredient. Ludo definitely seems to think so anyway, judging by all those times last year when she dragged me down here to giggle whenever he said "here's your white chocolate raspberry flapjack, ma'am". It's catching, that sort of giggling. And he is kind of decorative, what with the chestnut curls, and the cheekbones, and the way he holds his pencil in his mouth like a puppy when his hands are full. I get to play Mop Bucket Roller Hockey with him when we clear up at the end of the day (which he totally lets me win, sometimes). He's going to teach me how to make apple strudel. I even get talked to sometimes by The Lovely Safak, his very tall, very beautiful girlfriend, who I am in no way envious of.

I'm completely in love with someone else anyway. Mycroft Christie, my *very* favourite person in the universe.

Technically, he's not really a *person*. Technically, the debonair twenty-third-century time-travelling hero of the best! TV show! ever! *Mycroft Christie Investigates* is not actually going to turn up on my doorstep any time soon, to whisk me away to fangirl heaven. Mostly because he's time-trapped in present-day London pretending to be a detective for complicated plot reasons. And because he's obviously in crazypants love with his foxy arse-kicking sidekick Jori Song (with whom he fights crime and has Unresolved Sexual Tension). And also because they cancelled the show after three seasons, so now he only really exists inside my DVD player. But he's dashing, and charming, and conveniently available at the flick of a remote control, which is the sort of thing a girl finds handy when she's stuck with the Mothership and Dad Man's board game obsession for company all summer.

The two nice old ladies peer up at the new Wisdom, then into their teacups, looking slightly worried. The hiker guys just smile.

Betsy sees me watching them, and waits, expectant, chalk still in hand.

"French?"

"Belgian," she says gleefully, adding an extra strike under the score sheet on the blackboard. I am now losing "Identify The Tourist" by 31 points. Belgians: they get me every time.

Betsy slides me a slice of carrot cake, with a little fondant carrot on the top. Cinnamon, walnuts, orange peel, cream cheese. Squishy without being mushy; cakey without being dry: the kind you have to eat with a fork. Instant perkage. Maybe Teddy wasn't kidding about the secret ingredient.

I realize Betsy's hovering, watching me eat, and twisting her daisy ring. I suspect she wants to steal my fondant carrot.

"So . . . you sure you want to keep the Saturday job going, hon?" she says instead.

"Yep. Why wouldn't I?"

She leaves her ring alone and plucks at her fringe instead, making sure it's lying perfectly retro-flat. "It's been a great summer but . . . you've got exams this year. Maybe you want to party Friday nights. Maybe you, uh, might want to keep it to just outside of term time, you know? Give you a little more time with your buddies?"

UH.

HUH.

(Both allowed in Scrabble. According to Dad Man, anyway. I think he might be a CHEATER – 7 letter word, extra 50 points.)

I get it.

"You mean, do I want to avoid being the only kid at the Finch who needs to earn their pocket money?"

"I just thought it might be uncomfortable for you, honeybee. Serving your friends? Serving your non-friends, even?"

I shrug. "Actually, I'm kind of looking forward to that part. It'll be like *Friends*. They'll all come here to hang out, and I'll adorably get their orders wrong while having big hair."

Betsy smiles. "I see I have a lot to look forward to. Don't marry that Brad Pitt guy though."

5

"I'll try to fend him off."

"Feel free to fend him in my direction!" says The Lovely Safak, breezing through the door in a billowy summer dress. "Did you hear that, Teddy darling?"

"Yes, dear," calls Teddy from the kitchen. "I'm making jealous boyfriend faces back here, I swear."

"He's so well-trained," she whispers conspiratorially, slipping on to a stool beside me. "Not working today, Heidi?"

I explain awkwardly. The Lovely Safak goes to Mendip Road, the sixth-form college round the corner, and Mendies and Finches don't exactly mix. Safak's a bit above territorial fist fights in the Victoria Park fountain though. She just smiles, and wishes me luck.

"You sticking with this whole look for term time, too, honey?" says Betsy, waving up and down me with a fork.

"You mean The Coat? Oh, The Coat is definitely staying."

The Coat is my Thing right now. It's a raincoat: one of those belted beige ones that old pervs wear in parks to flash people. I found it in a cardboard box in the Finch garages after an afternoon's dust 'n' spider battling with Dad Man. I've decided it was left there by some ancient teacher who figured out the only way to escape the Goldfinch was to flee secretly in the night-time, leaving all his possessions behind. Old Stinky Mancoat sounds disgusting, I know, but I kind of like the way it skims the ground. It flaps out behind me when I'm on the Bike o' Doom in a not uncapelike, vaguely superheroic manner. It makes me feel very detect-y. I kind of love it.

The fact that Mycroft Christie wears one too is totally a coincidence.

"Well, I *love* it," says The Lovely Safak, continuing to be Lovely despite all my efforts to not like her. She even gives me a hug.

The two old ladies leave, so we embark on a game of "Advanced Identify the Tourist" with the remaining Belgians. (Plain old "Identify" got boring back in July when everyone was Australian for three days straight so we added an extra level, where you invent their lives as well. Betsy says it's a game people play on trains, to pass the time. I think she must mean American trains: doing that on a British one would probably get you stabbed. So Teddy does the pictures, Betsy and Safak come up with names and I do the making-up-crap-about-them. We created a whole life story for this one guy who came in every day for a week and only ever ordered soup: Dieter Jeter, Soup Eater. The strip of pictures is still pinned up behind the rows of mugs, with Teddy's weird scribbly cartoons of this guy with hair that kept mutating into whatever vegetable was in the soup that day. Yes, this is what people who work in cafes do to pass the time. Forgive us. We mean you no harm.)

The Belgian hikers become Hercules and Bertrand, a pair of sinister burglars whose maps reveal the route to heaps of pirate treasure buried beneath the Finch. They get immortalized in biro, pinned to the wall on the back of an order slip.

The Lovely Safak helps me eat more carrot cake.

Betsy lends me another Agatha Christie novel, continuing my mission to more fully detectify myself. I lend her the last disc of the *Mycroft Christie Investigates* Season 2 boxset, continuing my mission to share the Mycroft appreciation.

The Big Bean across the road fills up.

The Little Leaf stays weirdly quiet.

Then Betsy flips the NO TEA FOR YOU, SILLY LATE PEOPLE sign around on the front door, and starts to close up.

Dad Man drives up outside in his knackered blue van, waiting to take me up the hill for the first dinner, as promised.

It's time to go back to Finchworld. Time for real life to begin again.

The usual weirdnesses greet me. The discovery that Polly Cole has two matching smaller sisters of descending height, like Russian dolls, and a mum who would be the outside doll if she weren't the width of a pencil. Timo Januscz bursting into tears as his parents drive away. The Mothership, in her best purple velour tracksuit, waving at me like a loony as she drags a train of bored-looking couples in their best suits and going-to-church shoes off towards the lake.

"Hi, babes! Just giving some of our new parents the guided tour. This is *my* daughter, Heidi. She just loves it here at the Goldfinch, don't you, babes?"

I smile weakly. She's not exactly wrong though. I mean I could live without having to learn what co-valency means at 9a.m. on a Tuesday. I could definitely live without my Mothership being the person responsible for shouting "tuck in that bottom!" at me when I'm attempting gym class. But I'm going to have friends again, and we're going to hang out, and be gossipy (in a very intellectual, not talking about shoes kind of way), and be generally superheroic. Team Finch, Finch Force Four, the Leftover Squad are about to reunite for another term of thrilling adventures. The credits are about to roll, introducing Fili, enigmatic tech witch; Ludo, sexy-beautiful wildchild; Dai, the big guy with the heart of gold; and me, Heidi, the the fledgling detective whose geekiness is actually strangely attractive. Together we'll fight crime and/or homework, guided by our mentor Betsy, who'll supply us with our undercover missions via coded messages hidden in cupcakes. We'll have a theme tune. And costumes. We'll be completely awesome.

They don't actually know any of this yet, obviously. That's how undercover we are.

The Mothership leads the rest of the parentals away, and I head for the main entrance. There's a girl sitting on the top step of the

Manor, peeling an orange and dropping the skin into the pot of one of those weird square-cut hedges like green cubes on spikes, ruining the carefully constructed air of expensive perfection quite casually, like she isn't even trying.

"Good orange?" I ask.

Filicia Mathilde Diouf, the world's blackest Goth, scrunches up her nose. "Tart," she says.

"Same to you."

"Appreciated." She sucks on another segment: looks me up and down. "Nice coat."

"Detective," I explain.

She nods. Eats more orange. Flicks pips away with a flash of silver rings.

With anyone else, all these pauses would be awkward. But best friends don't need to do all that awkward "hi, missed you, how have you been" stuff: she says it all with that minute quirk at the corner of her mouth, which is very nearly a smile. And anyway, there's a shriek from inside the Manor house, echoing glassily off the walls of the corridor inside, funnelled out through the open oak doors, announcing the arrival of our resident noisemaker.

"HEIDIIIII!"

A human cannonball with invisible jetpack attachment flies out of the doorway and flings its skinny arms around me. Also hair. Lots of hair, all glossy and dark and a bit more in my mouth than is pleasant. I miss a few sentences while trying to escape. These little details do not worry Ludo.

". . . and the traffic was like AWFUL and I was totally UNPLEASED, because I wasn't even going to BE here, and there's like THE party tonight, and I have SO much to tell you before we even get to that, only you will SO not believe OH MY GOD, FILI! You're here! I didn't even KNOW you were here!"

Fili receives the hair-in-face treatment too. Ludo keeps talking. Fili rolls her eyes, and shoves a wet chunk of orange in Ludo's mouth.

Fruit: new weapon of choice.

Ludo squints as she swallows.

"Tart," she squeaks.

"Same to you," I say.

"She means it with love," says Fili.

"OH MY GOD I've missed you SO much!"

Ludo hugs us together again, and I find myself grinning like a loony.

Fili scoops up the orange peel from under the bush (which somehow she makes seem more rebellious than leaving it there) and we head inside to the Manor common room, with its squishy blue sofa and its plasma screen, to wait for Dai to complete the team.

A couple of hours later, once I can't see the TV for bodies, I realize I'm at the McCartney Party.

At the start of each term there's a blowout. The Upper School kids have to use up all the contraband hidden in their suitcases anyway before it gets confiscated, but the real prize is to get kicked out before school even begins – all in loving memory of STUART A. MCCARTNEY, 1979. McCartney is a legend. No one knows exactly what he did to get the boot. The story probably changes every year. But his name's on the Student of the Year board, carved into wood, painted gold and hung in the entrance hall where he stays, inspiration to all. The McCartney Party's not exactly invite-only: you just need to know where it is, and you'll only know that if you're the inviteable type. Usually it's in one of the Upper houses (the 16–18s, Stables for the girls, Lake for the guys): whoever got lucky enough to bag one of the bigger double bedrooms and has a roomie who doesn't mind people being sick in their bed. It's the thing everyone will be talking about tomorrow. It's the gossip textbook for the whole term.

And I'm at it. We're at it.

UM.

WOT?

This is not standard Heidi protocol. The Finch isn't exactly your average school, but it has its cliques, its little groups. The druggie kids in bands, the alky kids in bands, the Ana girls, the We Hate Everything crowd. Our cheerleaders are cutters with credit cards and police cautions but it's no different to any other school once you slice past the extra cash. Same rules everywhere. And the rules say that weirdass Leftover Squad Lower Schoolies do not get to play with the grown-up toys. Maybe Ludo might have sneaked in last year, back when she hung with the Pill Popettes. Maybe even doomy loomy Fili, when she was an emo. But never Big Dai, the fat gay kid in the corner. And definitely never me, the girl with the parents, the girl with the plaits, the girl who only ever hears about this stuff the next morning, after the Mothership's driven me back up the hill.

Maybe I've been watching too much *Mycroft Christie Investigates* lately, but it's possible there's a hole in the fabric of time and space, responsible for us being here.

The room is filling up now, starting to get crowded and stuffy. Bottles and cans of Coke get passed to the corner by the window, where, under cover of an armchair, Brendan Wilson tops them up from a glass bottle. Packets of crisps fly overhead. Jo-Jo Bemelmans brings in a stack of pizza boxes, and the smell of cheese and garlic takes over from the icky mix of perfume and hairspray. Scheherezade Adams swans in, all bounce and straps and brand-new nose.

I think about sneaking out, but Ludo's squeaking next to me, eyes big, reeling off a list of names under her breath like a butler at some fancy soirée. She's got her hand wrapped round my wrist, squeezing whenever someone especially significant goes by. It's not so bad, I suppose. I'm out of the habit of being squished in with so many other people, but really it's not that different from watching TV, in smellovision. And I'm in the perfect location to play detective. I'll observe the Finch species in its natural habitat: monitor behavioural patterns; take notes.

Timo Januscz is drinking alone.

Flick Henshall has reportedly locked herself in the second-floor loo in Stables. (Are these two facts related?)

Honey Prentiss has broken her arm, which may prevent her from playing the oboe all term. (Scheherezade looks quite pleased.)

Miyu Sugawara wants Oliver Bass to know that someone is a bitch, very loudly, just at one of those moments when the room falls oddly quiet. (NB: Anna-Louise Darbyshire's ULife photo page has been an impressive array of snog photos all summer, none of them featuring Oliver.)

And there are the newbies to check out, too: the ones who were just pretty or booze-equipped enough to get the McCartney Party auto-approval. A new Ana girl. Some guy with peroxide hair, a military greatcoat and piercings on his piercings, trying to eat pizza without snagging mozzarella on his spikes. A skinnyboy, all in black, that Fili's gone to talk to by the window, as if Goth radar is yanking them together – though actually he looks sort of familiar.

There's another new girl I almost miss, from the crowd around her, then from how almost-invisible she is in person. She's pale and gaunt and angular, arms and legs folded up and sticking out like some sort of insect, and wearing the sort of make-up that looks like it isn't make-up. I hear someone say "model". It computes.

"OH MY GOD," breathes Ludo. "Yuliya Kusnetsova? She's, like, EVERYWHERE. She did, like, *Vogue* Italia two months ago? She's HUGE."

She's kind of the opposite, but I let it slide. The name's familiar anyway.

"I think she's Fili's new room-mate," I say. "They've got that big double on the top floor of Manor, upstairs from you?"

Ludo gets her death-grip on to my wrist again.

"NO! Oh My God. Seriously? OH MY GOD. That is . . ."

"Awesome?" I suggest.

"TOTALLY!"

Somehow I'm not sure Fili will be so keen. But before I can drag her away from Gothboy to ask, I feel a tug on one of my plaits, and then nearly fly off the sofa as a body leaps over from behind and drops into the empty space beside me.

"Ding ding, Ryder. All aboard."

Big Dai Wyn Davies: man mountain, king of the bear hug. Well, what's left of him. Dai didn't get to be Big Dai just from being six foot tall, and it looks like he's going to need a new nickname. Same stupid grin, same rubbish spiky blond haircut, entirely new body.

"Holy crap, Dai, the lions really did eat you."

He looks stupidly pleased. "Safari diet. Followed by masochistic gym torture." He flexes an arm at me. Bits of it stick out in a manner that is probably meant to be impressive.

"WHOA!" says Ludo, leaning over me to poke his biceps. "Personal trainer?"

"Yep. On whom I had the most pathetic crush, so hello, dedication! You likey?"

Ludo gives him a small round of applause. I wrinkle my nose.

"You look like someone Photoshopped your head on to a lifeguard."

"I'll take that as the compliment you *obviously* intended it to be. *Betch*. You're looking majestic yourself, by the way. Loving the coat. Very . . . distinguished?"

I look down at myself. The Coat has started to seem a bit more bizarre now there are quite so many other people here to see it. In fact, now I'm paying a bit more attention, everyone else seems to be dressed a teensy bit more appropriately for a party. Not just the Upper kids who always look like that, all swingy hair and glitter make-up for 9 a.m. Biology, either. I mean *everyone*.

Fili doesn't count: aside from her being crazy-beautiful already, it is Goth Law never to be seen without the uniform and the face. And Ludo is always perky, and pretty, and strung about with jingly sparkly things. But she's different somehow: just a few slim gold threads around her wrists and neck instead of that ever-increasing cuff of grubby neon plastic bangles she had last year; golden streaks in her smooth dark hair; red lips instead of peachy pink. Dai's got new threads to go with his new absence of stomach too: magenta polo shirt with the collar flipped up, low-slung jeans so there's a wide line of boxers showing. He's even wearing man-jewellery: some tourist junk from his holiday, beads with a bit hanging down shaped like a tooth.

Pod people.

My friends have been replaced by Pod people. Robots. Zombie doppelgangers from space. The Leftover Squad has been hijacked by evil clones, and we haven't even been given our first mission yet.

OK, rewind that thought. I have no moral objection to people looking nice. I might not be exactly managing it myself, in my baggy jeans and my superdork plaits, but that just makes me the poster child for not being fooled by the advertising: it's what's inside that counts, don't judge a book, etc. It's what comes with the extra layers of lipgloss and perfume that's spooking me. Ludo finally lets go of my wrist, but only to do a quick hitch-and-jiggle on her bra, tugging her vest top down a notch as she eyes Scheherezade. Dai's telling me some story about lost luggage on the way to Madagascar, but the whole time he's looking around, eyes sliding up and down, approving and disapproving. Even Fili is tinkering with her braids, eyelashes fluttering shyly as Gothboy tries on her favourite ring with the spider on it.

It's catching. Everyone's doing it. I don't think there's a person in the room actually enjoying themselves: they're too busy checking each other out.

Not me though: the eyes hit, connect and slide on by.

Maybe my fledgling detective geekiness is not so attractive. Maybe I've got the casting for the Leftover Squad all wrong. I'm the comedy sidekick who falls in poo. The talking dog. The redshirt who gets killed off in episode 4, and no one really minds.

"This is SO awesome," whispers Ludo loudly in my ear.

OAR.

SUM.

I nog: nod and shrug, both at once.

Half an hour later, with the sky dark outside and nothing but MTV on the plasma screen to light the room, I realize I'm not dealing with zombie robot doppelgangers. It's the love potion episode. Every TV show has it sooner or later. Magic spell, monster bite, something in the water; romantic kryptonite that makes people lick faces with people they shouldn't. Mycroft Christie ended up snogging a vampire, an evil old lady who trained exploding hamsters to break into banks, and Jori Song (twice) while under the influence of bad mojo. Hilarious consequences generally ensue.

It's not so entertaining when you're in the middle of it.

OK, there's not exactly a Roman orgy happening. People are still wearing clothes, so far as I can tell from the flicker of the TV. It's pre-watershed, family-friendly, PG13. But everywhere I look it's going on. Tongues and hands and giggles in corners. Oliver Bass is proving how over Anna-Louise he is by sticking his tongue down Miyu's throat. Scheherezade is sitting on Jo-Jo's lap, arms draped over his shoulders. Brendan Wilson is sliding a hand up the new Ana girl's thigh, while she coyly smiles and fiddles with the hem of her skirt.

I hear Fili's laugh over the music, and see her curled up and cosy with her boytwin, holding hands, shoulders pressed together. I go to nudge Ludo and realize she's otherwise occupied, the peroxide-haired pierced newbie guy's mouth on hers, his hand resting, as if by total accident, on her boob. I squint my left eye closed, trying not to look, but I can still hear a vague slurpy noise. I turn to grab Dai, but the seat next to me is empty. I finally spot him in the corner near the door, dancing with Henry Kim and looking like he's won the lottery (which he kind of has, in Finch Gay Quarter terms: Henry Kim is famously cute, rich, and smart, and Dai has been lusting from afar as long as I've known him).

The Coat suddenly feels too appropriate, in all the wrong ways. I'm an accidental perv, trapped here staring at a roomful of people getting it on, because there's not really anywhere else to look. The only other person in the room who isn't coupling up (or trying to) is Model Yuliya, who is yawning over her can of Diet Coke and flicking through a magazine.

I check my watch. I begged and pleaded until the Mothership promised I could stay until 9.30 tonight. It's only just after 8.

I remember my purple patchwork bag's at my feet, and wonder if now would be a good time to whip out Agatha and read.

OK, that's *definitely* not the strangely attractive kind of geekiness.

I could go and find Dad Man, in his little cubbyhole of an office. Though at this time of year that'll probably mean helping him get all the trunks into storage. The Mothership might have finished already, setting up down at the pool: she could leave early, take me back down the hill to my poky little attic bedroom. I could watch the *Mycroft Christie Investigates* Season 3 finale again, in bed, with that White Magnum bar that I sneaked into the shopping trolley while the Mothership was fussing over whether bananas counted as Amber on her Traffic Light diet regime.

I reach down for my bag to get my phone, and when I come back up the seat next to me is no longer empty. Etienne Gracey. He's a Shroom, or he was: one of the Lower School bands, though he must be Upper School now. They played at the End of Year Ball. He sang.

"You're Heidi, yeah?" he says, shouting, over the music. He's leaning in very close.

"Etienne, right?"

He smiles, nodding. I can see a little frost of stubble on his chin and his upper lip, glowing blue then pink in the video light. I feel something touch my back, and try not to jump. It's his arm, sliding along the back of the sofa.

"Let me get you a drink," he says, and the arm disappears from my back.

"Oh My God, Heidi!" whispers Ludo in my ear, apparently coming up for air. "You are SO lucky! He's like so TOTALLY gorgeous."

I suppose he is. I mean, he's not as pretty as Teddy. Not

anywhere near as pretty as Mycroft Christie. But he's sort of a Finch pin-up. He's dated Scheherezade. And now he's settling back on to the couch next to me, pressing a can of Coke into my hand and sliding his arm back into position.

Ludo's elbow jabbing me excitedly in the rib area is not helping me to get my brain around this scenario, but Peroxide Guy distracts her again with a little more casual hand/boob interfacing and it's like we're alone together, me and Etienne.

Heidi and Etienne.

Is this how it works then? You just kind of sit there and wait for some boy to turn up and kiss you? I've been serving cups of tea to nice old ladies all summer: this all feels ultra-weird. But I suppose it's OK. It'll get it out of the way. I'm not fourteen any more. I'm fifteen. This is what fifteen-year-olds do.

I take a sip out of my can, and try not to cough as the whatever-it-is goes down. I don't really do alcohol. I'm probably drunk already.

"Thanks," I say, tilting the can at him.

Etienne just nods, bobbing his head slightly as the music changes. Madonna, thrusting her scary manlegs at me, in a not-especially-sexy kind of way.

I drink some more, in case my mouth tastes of carrot cake still. Because Etienne's going to kiss me. I think. I wonder if he'll feel prickly. I suppose he is quite pretty, up close.

Maybe you don't just sit there and wait? I didn't see anyone else having trouble getting to the kissing part of the evening, but I'm definitely doing something wrong. Talking, maybe? Are we supposed to do that first?

"So . . . any new Shrooms songs since last year?"

"Shrooms? We split. Creative differences, you know? I'm working on some solo material now though." He snarls at the TV screen. "Real music, y'know?"

"Mhmm," I say into my Coke. "I'd love to hear it. Sometime. If you like?"

"Yeah?" He keeps bobbing his head. "Cool."

The ultra-weird keeps on growing. I think I just asked him on a date, sort of. This is not standard behaviour. This is not Heidi. There actually really truly is love potion floating in the air, making everyone moronic, and I am not immune after all.

"So, your dad is, like, the security guy at night, yeah?"

"Night porter, yep." I try a goofy shrug. "Kind of embarrassing."

"What? Oh, yeah, I guess. Anyway, me and the guys were wondering: could you, like, distract him tonight or something?"

I look up, and see "the guys" hovering behind Etienne, looking hopeful. Big looming Upper Schoolers from Lake. Dave something, Jules Harper, some guy I don't know at all.

"The *real* McCartney Party's supposed to be up in Toni's room in Stables, only she says your dad was like patrolling all over down there, so we ended up down here with the kiddies in Baby House." He waves his can at the room, eyerolling. "No offence."

I swallow a big gulp, and taste the whatever-it-is, sticky on my teeth.

"No offence, yep," I mumble.

"So could you, like, go pretend to be ill or something, just to, like, keep him busy or whatever?"

He leans in again, arm still round my shoulder, fingers just lightly stroking the top of my arm.

"Sure," I hear myself say. "Whatever."

"*Awesome.*"

He gives my arm a squeeze, hops off the sofa, and he and "the guys" vanish.

OAK.

HEY.

Emergency Protocol #4. Ejector seats engaged. Alert, alert, incoming. When I say run, run.

I fumble for my bag, but Ludo's amazing ability to get her face snogged off and still see what's going on next to her is still in place. Her hand closes round my wrist again. I pull away, vaguely shaking my head, and climb over various writhey wriggly arms and legs to get out, out into the corridor.

It's cool and bright. No sweaty people, no stinky pizza, just a nice ordinary school-like corridor, with a noticeboard about netball practice times, and when the nurse will be available. The real world, back where I know the rules.

Ludo bangs the door on the unreal world of the common room, and scoots up to dangle off my shoulder, eyes like two fried eggs.

"Oh My God, what WAS that? I mean, WHAT? I mean, OH MY GOD!"

"Ryder, baby, what gives?"

Not-So-Big Dai appears, his face pink, a huge smile on his face, Henry close behind him.

"I KNOW! He was like all over her, and then FOOM, GONE."

"Etienne Gracey. Heidi, you *turned down* Etienne Gracey. That's . . . that's a parallel universe." Dai remembers Henry lingering at his shoulder. "Sorry. I didn't mean . . ."

Henry shrugs. "It's Etienne Gracey. No offence, but I'm right there with you."

Ludo grins her tiny pearly grin at me. Then her eyes suddenly get wider. Huge. Fried eggs times twenty. She starts swatting her hands, slapping her palms against me and Dai like we're on fire, and making little squeaks.

"OH MY GOD. I get it. I totally get it. Don't you get it?"

Dai looks at Henry. They don't get it.

I don't get it either. So much for my fledgling detective skills.

"DUH! Only possible explanation? She's totally SEEING someone already."

Dai gasps. Actually gasps.

"No!"

"TOTALLY. Right, Heidi? Right?"

Before I can get a word out, Ludo wraps her arms around my tummy and hugs me so hard I feel my elbows click. Dai joins in, pressing my head into his shirt. Henry wraps a cashmere-clad arm round me too, even though I don't really know him well enough for hugging, and the three of them squish me even tighter, with Ludo making small "eee" noises and jumping up and down.

"Anything of interest?"

They break off. Fili's leaning on the wall, Gothboy just behind, looking bemused.

"Ryder here has just turned down the tongue services of one Etienne Gracey, on account of having – drumroll, please – a secret boyfriend."

Ludo nods her head superfast, mouth wide open.

Fili quirks a brow. "Seriously?"

I look at Ludo, lipstick smeared into a doughnut round her mouth. I look at Dai, Henry's hand resting ever so casually on Dai's belt. I look at Fili, and how close Gothboy is standing, fingers twining in hers.

The Leftover Squad's new line-up.

Well, honestly. What would you say?

Recipe for an Imaginary Boyfriend

Ingredients:

A name

A haircut

Eyes (two, of improbable colour: seafoam green, topaz, etc.)

Stylish yet attainable clothing

An adorable "How We Met" Anecdote

Reasons why he is loveable

Reasons why he thinks I am loveable

Reasons why he is very far away and unlikely to phone me up

Hobbies (NOT SCRABBLE)

Method:

- Procure ingredients from Heidibrain
- Watch lots of *Mycroft Christie Investigates* for valuable insight into boylike behaviour
- Shape the mixture into vague appearance of Monsieur Le Sexay (exact biological accuracy not required, let's not even go there)
- Snog (imaginarily)

"An imaginary boyfriend?" Betsy breathes in through her nose. "OK. That's . . . uh. . ."

"The most amazingly brilliant idea in the history of the universe?"

"I was going to say 'creative', honeypie. But hey, he's your imaginary lovemonkey. Maybe you've seen a side to him I'm missing."

I sigh, and deliver a trayload of scones and tea to a concertina-spined elderly couple by the Little Leaf window. The place is deadsville again. Even the Daily Wisdom (TODAY'S MUFFINS ARE ROUND FLAT BREADY THINGS: *those other ones are just cupcakes with egos*) seems a bit glum. The first week back in Finchworld hasn't been a breeze either. Prowse has already rejected my Poem on an Autumn Leaf homework and demanded I do it again for next week, on pain of being put on report to Mrs Kemble, the Demon Headmistress. The Mothership's decided we're on a Red Foods Only phase, now Dad Man's back to sleeping up at the Finch six nights a week and isn't around to demand fish fingers and chips. The post-McCartney Party fallout is still ongoing, what with Etienne Gracey glaring at me for failure to distract, Jo-Jo Bemelmans getting busted with a pillowcaseful of empty vodka bottles, and Flick Henshall having ended up in a clinic after having her stomach pumped. Dad Man had to drive her out there at 4 in the morning. He looked all stringy the next day. I'm sworn to secrecy, of course, which in reality means I have to sit there pretending I know nothing while everyone else talks about it, because Flick Henshall does this about twice a term, and her completely empty bedroom is sort of a giveaway. Basically, my own parents are making me lie. No wonder I'm entering the subterfuge business.

"We going to have the company of the gang from up on the hill today?" Betsy asks, dusting invisible crumbs off the green velvet sofa, as if that'll magically make some customers appear on it.

"Not sure if they'll make it, actually. They're all pretty busy. With, you know, homework. And . . . stuff."

Betsy peers out at me from beneath her fringe, narrows her

eyes, and pointedly sets us up with a large pot of English Breakfast.

"Feeling a little left behind, hon?" she says gently.

OK, maybe not that good. She's a bit clever, Betsy.

"It's just not how I pictured the first week back, that's all."

I don't know what I pictured, really. It's not as if, over the summer, the Mothership suddenly realized that she did want to live in the staff housing behind Stables, where I could spend my evenings being exposed to Bad Influences and Extreme Teenage Behaviours. Or that our little flat magically flew over the ring road, so at least I'd be allowed to come home at curfew on the Bike o' Doom, by myself. I was always going to be stuck back in the attic every night. But I did have plans, for when I wasn't being Cinderella. Sneaking up to the dorm rooms (where Non-Resident Students – i.e. me – aren't supposed to be allowed) to lie on Fili's bed, IMing from one side of the room to the other. Making them all watch *Mycroft Christie Investigates* so we can fangirl him together. Watching kittens on YouTube and eating toast. It doesn't even sound all that good now. I just remember really looking forward to it, all summer. And somehow I forgot they might want to be doing other things, with other people.

I pick up the tufty end of my left plait, and glare at it. "It's like everyone else got a different script, you know? And I'm having to make it up as I go."

"Including a boyfriend?"

"Including a boyfriend. And don't look at me like that! It's not because I'm jealous. I think it's nice that all my friends have hooked up with people. They're happy, I'm happy."

That part is totally true. Dai's so giddy he keeps walking into doorframes. Ludo is even squeakier than usual. Fili and Gothboy float around in matching outfits (and since Gothboy has turned out to be Simon Grove, who last year was a wispy blond guy in a Jesus Saves T-shirt who used to fall asleep a lot in Maths, his transformation into her perfect twin seems like some extra-special romantic gesture). It's kind of amusing to observe.

Betsy's still looking unconvinced.

"It's OK to be single, honey. Just because everyone else is doing it doesn't mean you have to rush on after them."

"I'm just mucking about, honest. It's not like I set out to make up a boyfriend. Ludo got the wrong idea; I didn't put her right. Actually it's pretty entertaining, working out what he should be like. Like . . . pick 'n' mix. Only with body parts."

She's smirking now. "OK, honey, I'll buy it. I wish my first boyfriend had been imaginary. Then I could go ahead and unimagine him again. Along with the acne, and the poison breath, and the creepy kid sister who used to stare in at us through his car window. . ."

"See? This is why it's the most amazing idea ever. Imaginary Boy is not going to have any of those."

After all, I am kind of an expert at this. I've been having imaginary boyfriends since I learned how to turn on a TV. So far, I've had romantic shenanigans with:

The Milkybar Kid (I was eight: he was a. equivalent to me on the dorkage scale and b. had chocolate; b. was totally the clincher)
The kilt-wearing man on the porridge oats advert (KILT! No further explanation required)
Gok Wan (*sigh*)
Peter from Narnia
Ellen Page (obligatory girlcrush)
Peter Petrelli (shirtless)
MYCROFT CHRISTIE ♥

I'm practically a slut. Etienne Gracey would probably turn me down all over again, due to my intimidating sexual prowess.

"So, does he have a name? Because 'Imaginary Boy' is kind of a giveaway, hon."

"Still working on it."

Names are surprisingly tricky. All of the good ones are taken. And I can hardly call him Mycroft. I don't think my imagination is up to fake-dating a Mycroft, let alone anyone else's.

"Anything but Rupert!" comes a muffled voice from the kitchen.

Teddy. Teddy, who is usually still asleep at this hour of the morning creating his beautiful extra-fluffy curly bedhair. Fabulous tousled Teddy who is apparently not asleep, but in the kitchen, listening to my pathetic lack of a life.

ODE.

EAR.

Then again, he's also Teddy who is secretly not a Teddy at all, but a Rupert. (Betsy thought it sounded like a nice British name until they moved here and found out it translates locally as "hit me, hard, many times". There aren't even any Ruperts at the Finch. So: Rupert, Rupert Bear, Teddy.) He's kind of touchy about it.

"I've got an outstanding How We Met Anecdote all mapped out, though," I say, quickly, because Betsy's starting to look unconvinced. "Can you check it for plot-holes? Because Ludo's starting to invent her own version, and I'm running out of enigmatic coy looks."

"Have at it," she says, pouring more tea.

I settle myself on the stool, and take a deep breath.

"OK, so, we met at Paddington station. Buying jelly babies. I mean, I was buying jelly babies. Only I was running late, and I heard the train arrive so I ran for it, and I must've left my purse in the shop when I did, because just as I was about to get on the train someone grabbed my arm. And he was all breathless because he'd been running to catch up with me, so he couldn't get the words out to say 'here is your purse', and then the train doors went BEEP BEEP BEEP and closed, and the train left, and we were both just stood there. And he went 'you missed your train', and I went 'nnnnnnnngh' because he was all tall, dark and leather jackety. And holding my purse, which is the purple felt one with the flower on it that's falling off a bit. So he gave it back to me, and I said 'thank you', and probably our fingers brushed together with sparks of electricity – though I might skip that bit? – and we were just stood there, on this train platform, just the two of us. So I offered him a jelly baby, and he said 'only if I can have a red one, they're the best', and I said I liked the green ones best anyway, and then we just carried on talking, and la la la snogs, the end."

I take a big swig of tea.

"So what do you think?"

"Adorable," says Betsy. "A little too adorable, maybe? But hey, that's what fantasies are for, right?"

"I could ditch the jelly babies?"

"I like the jelly babies. Nice detail."

"The ending needs a little work."

"Yeah, but still, it's a good beginning. *Love* the leather jacket."

"OK, stop, I can't take any more!"

Teddy appears in the kitchen doorway, tousled bedhair in place (lightly dusted with flour), apron on over the top of stripy pyjama trousers and monster-feet slippers.

"Nobody's going to give a crap about the leather jacket and the jelly babies," he says, wagging a spoon at us and dripping icing on the floor, "not when the rest of it doesn't make any sense. Heidi, if you left your purse in the shop, how did you get through the turnstile on to the platform? Are you at Paddington *train* station or *underground* station? What are you even doing in London? I mean, don't you have somewhere to go? Doesn't he? And seriously, if some strange guy steals your purse and grabs your arm at a train station you want to push him on to the tracks, not kiss him. Just a suggestion."

"My son, the death of romance," sighs Betsy as Teddy heads back to the kitchen.

"Nope, he's right. It's not exactly realistic, is it?"

I decide not to mention the previous draft versions I came up with in Chemistry, when I was meant to be doing experimental things with potassium permanganate. There were pirates. And giraffe-riding. And he had a beret.

Apparently imaginary boyfriend-construction is harder than it looks.

"Maybe you should keep it simple," Betsy offers. "There doesn't need to be fireworks. Just go with something you'll be able to remember. Something familiar, you know?"

I spend the total lack of a lunchtime rush contemplating alternative locations for Imaginary Boy to share my jelly babies. Then I decide he (Michael?) is a vegetarian, and so we strike up a conversation about how jelly babies contain bits of dead cow. Then I decide that discussing bits of dead cow is probably not the ideal date conversation, and actually that he (Mikhail) is kind of a jerk for even mentioning it, in fact, ruining my jelly babies, and who does he (Mickey) even think he (Mikey) is, coming and hassling me in the park.

By the end of the day, I've dumped him (Artemis) about seventeen times, before we've even properly met. And he still doesn't have a name that isn't stupid.

"Inspiration for you," smiles Betsy as we close up early, sliding me a paper bag along with the little brown envelope of cash that I really obviously haven't earned.

"What's this?"

I peer inside the bag and find a warm solid gingerbread man, his iced-on eyes and buttons still slightly soft.

Betsy looks innocent.

"The Perfect Boyfriend. And he's not even imaginary."

When the Mothership and Dad Man first told me they'd got jobs in a boarding school, I had visions of a big Hogwarty castle with dining hall to match: oak panelling, portraits of dead people, feasting on wild boar by candlelight. The Finch dining hall is strip-lit, smells of beans and looks a bit like a posh McDonald's. The food is just as enticing: Oil Pie, Lettuce in Soup and the ever-popular Armoured Pizza. If the Mothership's Red Peppers stuffed with Red Lentils, Red Onion and Red Cabbage doesn't kill me, Fish Surprise is guaranteed to finish the job.

I line up with my plastic tray, but today there's not a lot left, and somehow I end up with nothing but four different kinds of potato on my plate by the time I've made it through the servery. I grab an apple (green, just to add to my Traffic Light rebellion), then weave through the tables, following the sound of Ludo's giggles.

Our official Leftover Squad corner is looking a little crowded these days, even with Ludo sitting on Peroxide Eric's lap wrapped up in the ends of his military coat, and Fili and Simon sitting so close together they might as well be sharing one chair.

"Ryder!" shouts Dai, waving me over. "At long last. We were starting to think you'd turned into the invisible woman."

Henry stands at once, and offers me his seat.

"Isn't that the mysterious Yuliya's job?" he asks, lounging against the back of Dai's chair while Dai beams with pride.

Yuliya, the stick-insect Russian model, has managed to not turn up to a single class I'm in so far. I'm starting to think I imagined her too.

"OH MY GOD, like, leave her alone?" Ludo flicks her hair, not noticing that some of it is now tangled in Peroxide Eric's nose-ring. "She probably has to sleep a lot to maintain her complexion."

"She's not going to come in here anyway," says Dai, hovering a hand over my plate and deciding to steal my apple instead. "Models don't eat. Well, not food."

I waggle Potato Variety #1: The Soggy Chip at him. "Don't think this qualifies."

"That is SO stereotypical," says Ludo, swinging her hair again.

There's a faint groan from behind her. I wince on Peroxide Eric's behalf. He gives me a grateful grin as he disentangles himself.

"I'm just saying she's probably got her reasons, which are probably, like, none of our business? And she's Fili's new roomie, you know? So we should TOTALLY be making her feel welcome."

"Very true," says Dai through a mouthful of apple. "So what *is* she like then?"

We all look at Fili.

Fili shrugs. "She's all right," she says eventually.

We wait, but that seems to be all we're getting.

"Simon? Anything you'd like to add? Like, actual information of some kind?" says Dai.

Simon frowns and says slowly, "She has really big hands."

"Ladies and gentlemen, the Finch gossip scandal of the year."

"Unless there's a thrilling story about how he found out she has really big hands?" suggests Henry, nudging Dai with his elbow.

Simon frowns again, blinking anxiously at Fili through his wispy black hair. "I just . . . looked."

Dai sighs heavily. "It's so worthwhile, knowing the people with the inside scoop."

"She's doing PAG," says Fili softly.

"OH MY GOD!" squeaks Ludo, eliciting another pained grunt from Peroxide Eric as he rubs ruefully at his ear. "Really? That's so awesome! We'll be, like, best friends! There'll probably be press photographers coming to see it and everything!"

I stab a lump in my grey mash. "PAG?"

"Performing Arts Group," says Henry. "We put on the Wassail show? With Venables?"

I nod. Everyone was still talking about the Wassail show when I arrived last January. It's the Christmas play really, but the Finch likes to think it's progressive and embraces all cultures (as long as they can pay the fees), so they can't call it that. There are still photos all over the music rooms, of the Main Hall set up with the posh auditorium seating that sort of folds out of the walls, with Henry in a purple cloak peering out from behind a curtain, and Big Dai dressed up as the Cowardly Lion. Dai looks more like a Cowardly Koala, but there's a Tin Man and a Scarecrow and Gillian Gerhardt in gingham, so I'm assuming the continental detour was an accident. And I know Venables, even though I've managed to escape his classes so far. He's got a little love posse who follow him round adoringly and quite possibly leave apples on his desk. Even the Mothership's always going on about how hilarious he is in the staff room. I don't really get it: all I see is one of those teachers who wears skinny jeans even though he's going bald, wants everyone to call him Phil and likes to sit cross-legged on the floor so he can "feel the vibe, man".

"Auditions next Wednesday," says Dai.

"Can you believe there were only, like, TWENTY places on the sheet for the Lower School? And you just KNOW that Scheherazade Adams was going to put herself down for, like, ALL of them."

31

"But Mr Venables!" lisps Henry, tilting his head into a scarily accurate impersonation, only with a bit less cleavage. "It simply wouldn't be fair on the people who've bought tickets if I didn't play heroine and hero! It's *so* much more modern that way."

"Don't worry, Ryder, I signed us all up."

Peroxide Eric sweeps Ludo's hair aside, and raises a hand. "Not me. Not exactly my scene."

It's not exactly my scene either. I give good audience. I am well trained in the art of viewing. Participation, not so much.

But maybe that's the old Heidi talking. I'm Heidi-with-a-boyfriend. Heidi-with-a-boyfriend could be in a play.

"They have non-speaking roles," says Fili softly.

"Scenery, lighting, music. . ." Dai has his best encouraging face on.

"Costume!" bellows Ludo, tugging on The Coat gleefully and nearly yanking my head off.

I squish down the tiny inner mumble of disappointment that even Heidi-with-a-boyfriend is not expected to wow the school with her undiscovered acting talent. A good detective should be watching from the wings anyway. It's like Mycroft Christie says in episode 1.11: *Noises Off*: *You can't see who's pulling the strings if you are one of the puppets.*

Dai's phone beeps. "Sorry, kiddies, must fly," he says, chucking my half-eaten apple back on my tray. "The weights room is calling. Time to get sweaty."

Henry smirks and murmurs something in Dai's ear.

"You can't go now!" Ludo's bobbing about on Peroxide Eric's knee like a five-year-old who needs a wee. "I know a thing about the thing!"

Fili glances at me, then gives her a stern look. "Ludo?"

"We're not talking about the thing," says Dai sternly. "The thing is none of our business, remember? Unless the thingee wants to share?"

They all look at me.

"I'm a *thingee*?"

"Oh, come ON," moans Ludo, her knees jiggling up and down. "The BOY? The super-mysterious secret boyfriend? The more-gorgeous-than-Etienne-Gracey boy we're all dying to know about WHOSE NAME I MIGHT HAPPEN TO KNOW?"

They all look intrigued. "They" includes me.

Ludo strangles me again, hauling on my collar and thrusting the inner lining of The Coat at Dai.

"HELLO? The coat OBVIOUSLY belongs to the super-mysterious secret boy because, duh, why else would she be wearing it? And what does it say in the coat?"

Dai loans in. I crane my head around to see the neatly sewn nametape under the hanging loop, that I've never really paid any attention to.

"Hartley," he reads.

"How romantic," says Henry.

Hartley. It sounds sort of familiar. I've probably seen it written there before without really noticing, the way you walk past the same row of shops all the time, but couldn't put them in order without them right in front of your nose.

"So, Ryder, does Hartley have a first name, or are you two sticking with the kinky boarding school thing?"

I take a deep breath.

They continue to all stare at me.

I can't do it, not lie straight to their faces. I'm coming clean. I'm telling the truth.

"Ed," I say. "His name's Ed."

I have no idea where it came from: the words just pop out

before I can inspect them for Paddington stationesque plot-holes. But I like it. I picture the little gingerbread dude Betsy gave me. I've saved him: propped him up on my bedside table, guarding Agatha Christie.

"Aww, look, she's gone all girly," squeaks Ludo, and I realise I'm grinning.

Ed Hartley. My boyfriend's name is Ed Hartley. Gingerbread Ed. EX.

SELL.

LENT.

Now he's got a name, the rest of the ingredients are going to just fall in my lap: I can feel it. I'm not just audience now. I get an executive producer credit. I'm the showrunner for *Heidi!*, the heart-warming yet hilarious tale of a plucky gal and her imaginary friend (not to be confused with that thing up a mountain, with goats).

Time for me to put my detective skills to work, starting with the basics: interrogation.

Mycroft Christie shines bright light in the eyes of the guys he's fleecing for information. I don't see why non-sentient baked people should be any different. I take the gingerbread man from his perch beside my Pinocchio alarm clock and prop him up against the base of my desk lamp. One of his eyes got a bit squished while I was bringing him home and he's starting to look sort of sweaty, but we can put that down to my intimidating detective demeanour. He still smells delicious though. I'd be tempted to eat him, if that didn't open up a whole can of associated dodge now that he's my boyfriend.

Interrogation #1 goes something like this:

A tiny cell. Heidi sits on her chair backwards. The gingerbread man stays standing, due to his legs not being bendy.

HEIDI: Hello, sexy. Please inform me of your vital statistics.

GINGERBREAD MAN: (enigmatic silence)

HEIDI: OK, perhaps the "sexy" thing is a bit forward. Please don't sue me for sexual harassment?

GINGERBREAD MAN: (enigmatic silence)

HEIDI: Although, come to think of it, you are technically naked, so we're probably about even on the inappropriate behaviour front.

GINGERBREAD MAN: (enigmatic silence)

HEIDI: So, what kind of music are you into? Who would win in a fight, astronauts or cavemen? Boxers or briefs?

GINGERBREAD MAN: (enigmatic silence: possible sarcastic expression)

Mycroft Christie makes this look easy. But he has a sexy leather-clad sidekick to help him. And maybe my Gingerbread Ed's like Mycroft: one of those stoic noble types who gets tied to a chair and thumped about once a week till he just wriggles prettily and then escapes.

Or maybe Mycroft Christie has just never tried to interrogate a biscuit.

OK, this is getting embarrassing.

FOE.

CUSS.

Betsy said to keep it simple. To stick to something familiar. I'm going about this all wrong: trying to come up with a brand-new imaginary person when I can just borrow one. Trying to *be* the hero, when the hero's what I'm hunting. After all, there's one person I already know inside out and backwards. And he's definitely the type to wear The Coat.

Interrogation #2:

A dimly lit penthouse, belonging to time-travelling gentleman detective Mycroft Christie. He returns home to find a young lady mixing him a cocktail: not his usual colleague Jori Song, but the equally foxalicious Miss Heidi Ryder.

HEIDI: Good evening, Mycroft. I'm from the Time Bureau, here to give you your new assignment.

MYCROFT CHRISTIE: Time Bureau? Madam, there's no such thing!

HEIDI: Ooh! That's from episode 1.4: *Lost in Metropolis*, the scene in the Chinese restaurant where the evil journalist woman tries to expose you. Right before you pour soup all over yourself so you can run away. I love that bit.

MYCROFT CHRISTIE: (attractive crinkly smile) It appears you know me rather well.

HEIDI: Episode 1.13: *Cavalry*, when it looks like you're about to tell Jori everything and then don't. And yes, I do know you rather well. Almost as if I'm some sort of scary obsessive fangirl with your entire life on DVD. Or something. Anyway, this new assignment. I need you to go undercover as my boyfriend.

MYCROFT CHRISTIE: I can't cook. I'm terribly afraid of the dark. I have a severe allergy to bee stings, shrimp and unrequited love.

HEIDI: Perfect! I am taking notes. No quoting from Season 3 allowed, though: that's when you grew The Horrible Beard. Ed can't have a Horrible Beard.

MYCROFT CHRISTIE: When I was just a little older than you, I fell off my hoverbike and broke my leg in three places.

HEIDI: No hoverbikes either.

MYCROFT CHRISTIE: I was nursed back to health by the most charming young woman.

HEIDI: Bingo! I smell a potential How We Met anecdote! You're pretty good at this. Any more?

THE MOTHERSHIP: Hi, babes!

MYCROFT CHRISTIE: (breaks chair over her head for interrupting)

HEIDI: Er. Don't do that. Well, do, but not right now?

We're not in a penthouse. I'm not foxalicious. And the Mothership is looking at me kind of funny, which is fair enough because I'm probably all pink-faced and ridiculous-looking, what with the talking to people who aren't there.

"I'm . . . rehearsing. For the Performing Arts Group. Auditions. This week?"

Actually that's quite impressive as explanations go. She seems pleased anyway.

"That's great, babes! Be nice to have you getting a bit more involved in school activities. Not stuck up here watching telly all the time."

I nog.

"I'll leave you to it, babes," she says, backing out. Then her eyes fall on the desk. The lamp. The gingerbread man, standing there trying to look innocent.

I think the Mothership just caught my boyfriend hiding in my bedroom. I feel so grown up.

"Hei-*di*," she says with a sigh. "I know you and your father think it's a bit silly, but it does help me to stick to it if you do it too, and I don't think he really fits my Traffic Light system, does he?"

"Well, no. But I haven't eaten him. He's . . . my inspiration. If I suddenly feel an urge for naughty Yellow foods on a Red day, I'll know he's watching. So just leave him there, yeah? Don't tidy him up or anything."

She smooths her hand down one of my plaits, tucking in the straggly bits, and makes one of those cutesy Mothership faces: tilt head, sigh.

"Everything all right, babes? Anything you want to tell me?"

I do want to tell her. *I've got this amazing boyfriend called Ed, who smells like cinnamon and looks like Mycroft Christie, and I don't even care how weird it is because just thinking about him makes me smile, just like Dai does when he talks about Henry, and Ludo does whenever Peroxide Eric sweeps into a room, and Fili and Simon do all the time, because they're never apart. Maybe even better than that.*

But she's the Mothership. She understands the rules of netball, but I don't think she's qualified to deal with Ed.

And anyway, I don't have to. I've got Gingerbread Ed, my little sentry on the desk, keeping all my secrets safe.

Now Ed's got a name and a face (I'm picturing a little more Mycroft than Gingerbread Man, though a bit younger, obviously), life is sweet. Now I'm primed to giggle along in any conversation, ready to throw in a casual little detail from my own love life. I'll have to do some editing, obviously, if anyone asks: Mycroft Christie's life tends to involve a few more fistfights with evil ninjas than the average person's does. Our first official date was a movie (though killer vampire bats didn't fly off the screen and start attacking people when me and Ed went). I've clung to his back as he rode Jori

Song's motorbike out into the country (although we weren't being shot at by the alternate-universe Evil Time Bureau). We've had very deep and meaningful conversations about life, and time, and responsibility (but we didn't always have to fit them into three minutes at the end of the episode).

It's like being undercover. I could be exposed at any moment, but only if I mess up and say too much. It's a total thrill.

It even makes ITP feel useful. ITP stands for Integration Through Positivity. Or Isn't This Pointless. It depends who you ask. Pottery and group hugs, to Promote Our Individuality, Embrace Our Diversity, and Capitalize Meaningless Phrases In General, all presided over by the frizzy-haired, ethnically beaded, fairtrade-coffee-drinking Mizz Cooper. Except that Mizz Cooper has gone on a yogic retreat in a tent somewhere where they make butter out of yaks for the whole term, leaving the hugs to be delivered by Mrs Ashe from the Science department. Mrs Ashe of the lumpy waist-height monoboob and the glasses-on-a-sparkly-string. The closest she's ever got to Cooperesque touchy-feeliness before was probably when she bought an organic banana by accident. It's like being told what periods are by the Queen.

At least I have Fili in my group this year. Plus Dai's Henry, and Peroxide Eric. I like the idea of getting to know them a bit better. And it's perfect for everyone getting to know Ed a bit better too.

Ashe sticks exactly to Cooper's lesson plans from last term, so after half an hour's team-building a meditation space out of eggboxes and cellophane we get to the Contribution. In other lessons, the Contribution is known as "that part where you actually have to write stuff down". This time, it's "Share a happy memory".

OUTS.

TAN.

DING.

We get ten minutes' writing time, then we have to read them out.

Brendan Wilson's definition of "happy" makes Ashe turn purple in the face, and rip the paper out of his hand before he can get more than three sentences in. Peroxide Eric has written about how much he likes pink fluffy bunny rabbits, Honey's is about buying a handbag and Fili has written HAPPINESS IS OVERRATED in eyeliner on her paper, and just holds it up instead of reading it out. I'm starting to feel daft for taking it seriously, but then it's my turn.

I feel happy when I think about my boyfriend Ed, and how we met. He was here on one of the Goldfinch summer courses for a few weeks, for physiotherapy, because he had an accident on his motorbike and hurt his knee. And all the other people who were here having physiotherapy were old women, so we kind of got talking this one time when I found him on the Manor steps playing "Lola" on his acoustic guitar, and then he stayed on for a few extra weeks just to hang out and talk about music and poetry and bikes, even after his knee was totally better. And now he's back in a different boarding school in London, so I won't see him for ages. But if I play that song I can still remember him sitting there, and it always makes me happy.

The "Lola" thing just came to me at the last minute. I have a moment of panic that I've pushed too far. But then Henry reads his, which is about watching Dai jogging round the lake at 6 a.m. when he thinks no one's watching, when there's still a layer of foggy cloud sitting on it. His voice is all warm when he speaks: he even gets a little flush in his cheeks. If it's good enough for Henry Kim, I guess being sappy and ridiculous is OK.

I'm in love, after all. I'm supposed to be a bit dorky.

It works anyway. By the afternoon, it's filtered back to Dai, who hums the chorus of "Lola" at me all through History.

By the next day, Ludo's started asking me questions about which school Ed's at, and where it is in London.

Sometimes my own brilliance can be a bit of a burden.

I'm lucky though. Ludo's pretty easy to distract, and Ed isn't the big event of the week. Wednesday is the first meeting of the Performing Arts Group, for the grand announcement of what the Wassail performance will be.

Dai grabs me at the end of French and marches me down to the Performing Arts Block on the far side of Stables. I've been in and out of the music rooms that lead off the foyer before, helping Dad Man move a bunch of weird African drums and jingly bells around over the summer. But I've never done more than peer through the windows at the auditorium itself. Venables is already flailing around on the stage, wearing a floaty white shirt that's got too many buttons undone. (Hairy chest. I make a mental note to keep Ed unfuzzy.) He's got his usual swarm of girlies in attendance, Scheherezade and Honey and Leila, flicking their hair and pouting up at him. There's a sort of smog of perfume in the air. Underneath it, patchouli oil and cigarettes, from the Upper School arts geeks. And that strange dusty smell of velvet seats, like an ancient cinema.

"Come on in, guys, take a pew," Venables yells, waving his arms and sending his if-I-keep-it-long-no-one-will-notice-I'm-going-bald hair flapping around his face. "Doesn't matter where you sit. Eat your lunch, pick your nose, do what you like, just need your attention thisaway. Brilliant. Love it. Brilliant."

Henry's already snagged us a row smack in the middle of the tiered seating and he waves me and Dai over. Fili and Simon are there already, locked in their usual inaudible conversation.

The stinky patchouli people sit in the row in front of us. The Venablettes take up position at the very front, sitting up perkily straight. Everyone's conversations slowly get quieter and quieter, as if someone's leaning on the volume control.

"Where's. . ." I start to whisper.

There's a bang and a clatter from the doors. Ludo, breathlessly dragging a bored-looking Yuliya behind her.

"That's it, come in, come in," yells Venables, beckoning them in as they squeeze on to the end of our row. "Plenty of room, folks. Brilliant. OK? OK. I think that's everyone. Let's get started, shall we?"

Total silence.

"Bloody hell, you guys are quiet! Can't have that. See lots of familiar faces here from last year, yeah? You guys know I don't do quiet. Theatre doesn't do quiet. Theatre needs you BIG and BRAVE, yeah?"

There's a mumble of "yeahs" in return.

"Can't hear you," says Venables, cupping his ear.

"Yeah."

"Still can't hear you! On your feet!"

The floor bounces slightly beneath my feet. Everyone stands up. I look up at Timo Januscz's arse: realize I'm the only one not standing. Dai gives me a look till I give in and stand up.

"Let's get moving, come on! Hands in the air! Waggle them round! Pat your knees! Roll your shoulders back! Roll them forwards! BIG and BRAVE, yeah?"

"Yeah!" yells everyone. Well, almost everyone. Fili is rolling her eyes as well as her shoulders. Yuliya is standing quite still, watching the whole thing with her mouth forming a perfect O of horror.

I decide I kind of like Yuliya.

"Heidi, come ON!" says Ludo over the chorus of "Yeah"ing, windmilling her arms. "You have to get into it properly!"

"Don't ever let me start a session without a warm-up, you guys, yeah?" bellows Venables, patting the air to tell us we can sit again.

"Can't expect your brains to work if your bodies aren't moving, right?"

I usually expect my brain to work *instead* of my body moving, but Venables is blethering something about "kinetic energy", and rifling through his man-bag. Finally, he triumphantly thrusts a cream paperback book with old-fashioned black lettering on it towards us.

"Anyone recognize this?"

"It's a book," I say automatically and a teensy bit louder than planned.

"A book?" Venables cups his ear again. "Yes! It is! Never be afraid to state the obvious, guys. Nothing's obvious, yeah? But not just any book! It's a play, called *Twelfth Night*. Pretty famous. The guy that wrote it's pretty famous too. The biggest celeb of the literary world? Shakespeare, guys!"

There's a vague murmuring around the auditorium.

"Come on, I know what you guys are all thinking. It tells us it's boring! Old Billy Shakespeare: words no one understands, nobody knows what's going on, everybody gets stabbed at the end, yeah?"

I have to give Venables a few points there. We did *Hamlet* in English last year. I liked his proto-emokid thing, but I did write an entire essay about how it would've benefited from being forty-two minutes long, and finished with a paragraph that read "In conclusion, NEEDS MORE JOKES". Prowse gave me a D.

People laugh, anyway.

"Well, don't all rush for the doors yet, guys, yeah? Because first off, *Twelfth Night* is about cross-dressing and gay sex. And second of all, this play? Billy's play? That's not what we're doing."

He chucks the book over his shoulder. Someone claps.

"We're doing. . ." There's more rifling of the man-bag. "This!"

He unrolls a poster with TWELFTH NIGHT: THE MUSICAL written in huge, crappy marker-pen lettering.

HOE.

CAY.

Venables grins like a mental monkey as mumbling starts up all over, and waves his arms a lot as he starts to tell everyone the plot. There are some impossibly identical boy–girl twins, and the girl dresses up like a boy, and a duke falls in love with him, which is apparently OK in Old Billy time because she's really a girl. Some guy wears comedy socks. And there's a clown.

"But forget all that stuff about dukes, guys. This is not 1601. No one is going to be wearing codpieces in this production. We're better than that, guys. We're going to set this somewhere crazy. Take our audience somewhere they didn't know they were going to go. Shake up our Shakespeare!"

Venables whips out a marker, and writes IN THE 80s on his flipchart, then adds !!!! on the end.

Fili makes a little moaning noise of despair.

"OH MY GOD!" hisses Ludo. "Legwarmers! And Lycra! And blue mascara!" From the look on her face, these are apparently supposed to be good things.

Then we're all filtering back out of the comfy seats into the foyer, to sign up for roles. The acting/singing people have to audition – not in front of everyone else, but I still wrestle the pen out of Dai's hand and cross my name off from where he's gleefully written it in. Detectives definitely stay backstage if there are going to be legwarmers involved. I hover over Set Design/Construction, but Timo and the patchouli gang are already signed up, and I'm not sure I can handle poetic wangst while standing on a ladder. Simon's name is under Costume though. I've never made anything more ambitious than my patchwork bag (and that's mostly held together with staples), but I always wanted to be one of those kitschy home-sewn kids. And Simon may need some assistance with colours that aren't black.

Costume it is.

The others are all on the audition pile, getting their stuff together to head back into the auditorium in little groups and sing Songs From Annie, or whatever people do in auditions.

"Costumers? Brilliant, brilliant," Venables yells, flapping his arms and wafting me and Simon over to him. "Love it, yeah? 80s. You know the 80s, yeah? Brilliant. Perfecto. And don't panic about construction, materials, budget, all that jazz. Right now I just want your creativity. You can come up with some concept artwork for me, yeah? This time next week? Brilliant. Love it."

And then he flails off to be scarily enthusiastic in the direction of the props department.

"Can you draw?" I ask Simon, hopefully.

He shakes his head, blue-black hair dangling in his eyes.

"Know anything about the 80s?"

He shakes his head again and picks a hole in his black nail varnish.

I'm starting to think signing up with uncommunicative Gothboy was not the most stellar plan. Especially when I can't draw and also know nothing about the 80s, apart from what I learned from TV. According to which the 80s were mostly very very gay. In helicopters. And short shorts.

Probably not what Shakespeare had in mind, but it's a start.

My phone goes off inside my patchwork bag, sending the *Mycroft Christie Investigates* theme tune twangling out across the room. I burrow in my bag. The caller ID reads *Mothership*.

I scrunch up my face, then scurry into the safety of Music Room 1 to answer.

"Babes? You're where? Oh. Right. You be good for Mr Venables now. What? Oh, yeah. Just wanted to remind you, I've got Girls' Aquarobics tonight, so you'll have to eat in the dining hall, babes, OK, and I'll pick you up after? Or if you'd rather wait there's my things in the fridge, but don't have the blueberries, I'm going all-blue tomorrow. Yes, I know traffic lights aren't blue. All right then, cheers, babes."

I perform a mental calculation involving the contents of my last pay envelope and the pizza delivery guy. The results are not good. Looks like Potatoes R Us for dinner again.

I shove the phone away and head for the foyer, knocking against a tubful of those spongy lollipop-shaped things you hit xylophones with, and spilling a few.

"Twenty says she's dumped," I hear Dai say, as I stop to put them back.

HELL.

OH.

I hang back for a little detecto-eavesdropping.

"You are SO mean! Ed totally wouldn't do that. Not on the phone, anyway."

"He's in London, Ludo. What's he going to do, sky-write? I'm just saying, he can't be that into her. He hardly ever phones. He doesn't even text."

"Perhaps she's not that into him?" That's Henry. Hooray for Henry. I think.

"Henry! She is TOTALLY into him. Like, OBSESSO."

"She doesn't have a photo of him in her wallet." Dai again. No hooray for him.

"You looked?"

"Just out of curiosity. None on her ULife profile either – which, by the way, still says she's single."

OOPS.

"Dai, sweetheart, I think you're the obsesso one."

"Henry, *sweetheart*, what's the background on your mobile phone?"

"A . . . picture of you and me."

"And Henry, *sweetheart*, how long have we been going out?"

"You may have a point."

"Maybe he's just too minging for her to want to look at."

"OH MY GOD, Dai, he is SO not minging!"

"How would you even know?"

I decide that's probably enough, and do a big notice-me-coming cough as I come out from my Music-Room 1 hiding place.

There's blushing and hair-tweaking and a general checking of watches, like the audition has already begun, and they're rehearsing Overplayed Pretending To Be Invisible. Apart from Yuliya, who has sat silent through the whole conversation as if it's very much beneath her (along with everything else), and Fili, who looks stony as always but is so, so amused on the inside. I think.

"Was that Ed on the phone, then?" says Dai, casual-like.

I nod.

"Everything OK?" says Ludo, looking hopeful on my behalf.

"He's . . . going through some stuff," I say, fiddling with my phone. "Having an identity crisis, kind of. It's a thing. No big. All fine. We're good."

Or we will be. Just as soon as I get my mental recipe book out again, and start cooking.

Recipe for a Non-Imaginary Boyfriend

Ingredients:

Frequent text messages o' love
Frequent phone calls o' love
Visibility in many photographs (preferably licking your face)
Presents
All the sexy sort of stuff
Actual existence in the real world

Method:

- Be in same room as non-fictional boyfriend
- Attempt to resemble octopus
- Repeat

I've been going about this all wrong. I get that now. I got all overexcited about the idea of me snuggled up in Mycroft Christie's coat, listening to him – I mean *Ed* – talking about his heroic detective exploits, and forgot that it wasn't really me that needed to hear it. After all, it doesn't matter if I don't love Ed at all, so long as everyone else believes I do.

The gingerbread man on my desk looks despondent.

OK, he doesn't. But he looks as if he might be thinking about it. I give him a reassuring little pat on the head.

I'm going to fix it anyway. I've constructed my pretty boy who falls off motorbikes and plays me songs on his guitar while tragically wounded. The basic recipe is awesome. Ed just needs to be a little more proactive, and a little less ten centimetres high and leaning on my desk lamp.

The "actual existence" thing I'm skipping, obviously. And with Ed being off in London (somewhere) at his boarding school (which has no name), he can't be expected to participate in any octopus action. I don't need to hand-write cute Post-it notes to be left inside my copy of *Deutsch Heute*, like Dai keeps leaving for Henry. He's not required to sweep up behind me, wrap his hands over my eyes and whisper filthy nothings into my ear, like Peroxide Eric. No sharing of mirror compact and the loan of dark cherry lippy, like Simon does for Fili.

All of which I'm completely fine with. Especially the lippy.

And thanks to the Mothership, I have the occasional phone call sewn up (so long as I can encourage her to ring me at random intervals, which will be easily achieved by me rearranging the fridge).

The rest, however, is a teensy bit more complicated.

I don't even know if you can text your own phone, but caller ID will not be on my side, and my Little Leaf wages are not going to buy me a whole new mobile. Betsy might be in on the plan, but asking her to send me little "ILU" messages would be beyond weird. So texting is out.

The Little Leaf wages aren't going to run to deliveries of red roses and posh chocolates either, and posting myself a bar of Dairy Milk isn't going to have quite the same effect – so pressies are out.

I can cut 'n' paste with the best of them, but a screencap of Mycroft Christie with my head Photoshopped on to Jori Song's is going to come out fugly. So the photo is out.

Which leaves . . . nothing.

And I've got to create a working scale model of the solar system out of drinking straws and bouncy balls, come up with those costume designs for PAG somehow, and write another Poem on an Autumn Leaf for Prowse.

It's impossible.

A dimly lit penthouse. Mycroft Christie, time-travelling gentleman detective, is admiring the view of the City of London. His delightful sidekick, Miss Heidi Ryder, is wearing pyjamas with giraffes on and looking sort of grumpy.

MYCROFT CHRISTIE: Nothing is impossible: only improbable.

HEIDI: Fancy seeing you here. And yeah, yeah, episode 2.1: *Ghost Town*, explaining to Inspector Dedman that ghosts could've done all those murders, which you'd think he'd know what with him being one. This is supposed to help me how?

MYCROFT CHRISTIE: The solution may be closer to home than you realize, Inspector.

HEIDI: What's that supposed to mean. Ed is a ghost?

MYCROFT CHRISTIE: No, Heidi, Ed is not a ghost.

HEIDI: Eh?

MYCROFT CHRISTIE: I said, *No, Heidi, Ed is not a ghost.*

HEIDI: But you don't say that. On the TV. In the show. You never say that.

MYCROFT CHRISTIE: I do now.

HEIDI: OK, I'm officially weirded out.

MYCROFT CHRISTIE: You're having an imaginary conversation with a character off the television. It took you until now to become "weirded out"?

HEIDI: Fair point. Actually this is kind of cool.

MYCROFT CHRISTIE: Of course it is. That's why you're making it happen, you dork.

HEIDI: Mycroft Christie would never say "dork".

MYCROFT CHRISTIE: Madam, you can make me say whatever you like. Bum. Wee-wee. I'm leaving that hussy Jori Song behind, my darling. Let's run away and detect things together!

HEIDI: Yes, please! Er, I mean, I couldn't possibly. I already have a boyfriend. And don't say bum.

MYCROFT CHRISTIE: Make me.

HEIDI: OK. Done. You are now bottomless.

MYCROFT CHRISTIE: Very clever. Now, might we apply the same principle to young Edward?

HEIDI: Ed? I don't think I want him to be bottomless.

MYCROFT CHRISTIE: I was referring to your skills of ventriloquism. If you can make me say whatever you like, you can make Ed say whatever you like too.

HEIDI: How does that help, if no one can hear it?

MYCROFT CHRISTIE: Your technology is rather unimpressive to a time-traveller like me, true enough, but I believe the Internet might offer some assistance?

HEIDI: Ooh. *Ooh.* Actually that could work.

MYCROFT CHRISTIE: Naturally.

HEIDI: But if I made you say that, then I must've known it already, before you said it. So technically it must be my idea. Right?

MYCROFT CHRISTIE: (pouty face)

HEIDI: (sighs)

He's right though. Or I am. You can be anyone you like on the Internet. You can even be two people at once. I can log into my ULife whenever (and sneakily update my status to "In a relationship", just in case Dai happens to check again). But I can just as easily start a whole new ULife, with whatever name I choose, and it's like creating a whole new person for all the world to see.

I fire up the Dread Pirate Laptop, and get creative with my new ingredients. Email address, username, profile. I hesitate over the Profile Image option, wondering if Photoshopped Mycroft Christie really is the worst idea ever; wondering if leaving it blank is just asking for suspicion. Then I catch the winking squished eye of my gingerbread man and whip out my phone. One blurry cameraphone upload later, and he's all set for public consumption.

ULife profile
gingerbread_ed <edmund.hartley@frogmail.com>
M, 17, in a relationship
Likes: my bike, my guitar, my Heidi
Dislikes: dairy products, knee surgery, Craphole Academy for Boys
Music: Dylan pre-65, Lennon, The Kinks, The Chi-Mos
Movies: Betty Blue, How I Won The War, Requiem for a Dream
TV: I don't watch much TV
Books: Ginsberg, Kerouac, Bukowski
Interests: riding the boulevard of broken dreams

The London penthouse. Miss Heidi Ryder is working hard at the desk, while Mycroft Christie, time-travelling gentleman detective, sulkily observes.

MYCROFT CHRISTIE: Edmund?
HEIDI: Only because edward.hartley@frogmail.com was already taken. I like it anyway. It sounds sophisticated.

MYCROFT CHRISTIE: Of course it does, my dear. And his disdain for television?

HEIDI: A cunning disguise so no one will guess he's me, mixed up with a few bits I borrowed off you.

MYCROFT CHRISTIE: Cunning indeed. Although your memory seems to be faltering: I believe, if you refer to episode 1.7: *Librarians Do the Funniest Things*, you'll discover that my favourite book is *The Tell-Tale Timesink*, by H.R. Pendellikon.

HEIDI: Shush. I am busy with my other imaginary boyfriend, whose interests are not allowed to be as made-up as yours.

I had to do quite a lot of Googling. But he seems like the kind of boy who might sit on the Manor steps and play songs to passing girls: the kind of boy the girls might stop and chat to, because of his effortless charm and good looks and knowledge of hipster writers I haven't read. Not the kind of boy who stops and talks to girls like *me*, anywhere but inside my crazy head. But that doesn't matter. They don't matter. I can make this Ed like me: that's all that counts.

He still needs to talk though.

I click on "Post to ULife" and hover my hands over the keyboard.

Subject: first post

Good evening.

Too formal.

Hey you guys!

Too Venables-esque.

hey

It's a typo, but I like it. It's his typing schtick: he's lower-case ed, too cool for the shift key. I can even go back and edit "ee cummings" into his "Likes" list, just for consistency.

heidi made me come on this site so i can talk to her because apparently i never do

OK, way to cast yourself as Whiny Girlfriend #1.

heidicakes has an account here so i just had to as well so i could tell her how gorgeous she is!!!

Ick. He's imaginary, not blind and delusional. And "Heidicakes"?

so i guess i should update this or something, since it's here, and i'm feeling kind of lonely.

This I like. He's melancholy, and nonchalant, and all those other things people only are in poems.

i guess h is the only one who'll read it anyway.

I like the "h" thing. No one's ever called me "h" before.

sorry for not phoning much this week, bb, got caught texting in media studies and mr smith has confiscated my mobile.

My boyfriend, last of the great rebels. (And Mr *Smith*? Come on, brain.)

sorry i haven't been calling much. been trying to get the bike running again, marco's got me some shifts at the garage, still doing physio. plus whenever i have to hang up it just reminds me how far away you are.

Yeah, baby. He's probably crying a Single Perfect Tear through the grease marks on his face as he sweats over his big foxy motorbike.

Too much?

Well, yes, but I don't care.

you'll only yell at me for trying to get back on the bike anyway, amirite? :P

Does Ed say :P?

you'll only yell at me for trying to get back on the bike anyway, right?

OK, he's going to have to say :P, otherwise it looks like we're having an argument, and it's a bit too soon in our relationship for us to be fighting.

how's tricks? am bored out of my mind already. new roommate guy continues to suffer personal hygiene issues.

Too prissy for manly motorbike boyfriend.

new roommate bilbo continues to smell. mostly of socks. think he has just the one pair. suggestions?

I start formulating cute banter immediately. Brilliant. We really are an adorable couple.

ok, getting dragged out of the door for a run. would bring laptop with me and keep typing, but i'm not quite that talented. (ok, i am exactly that talented, i just don't want to dazzle you from afar, it's too cruel.) thanks for the parcel. marco says "hello heidi like your picture nice to know he didn't just invent you to make his summer sound less crappy".

i have to go now so i can hit him on your behalf.

ok, really going now. miss you like tuesday afternoons,

ed

The penthouse. Mycroft Christie, time-travelling gentleman detective, leans over Miss Heidi Ryder's elegant shoulder to assess her work.

MYCROFT CHRISTIE: A commendable effort, young lady. The validation of your story from the mythical "Marco" is particularly astute.

HEIDI: Why, thank you. I like the way I've sent him an invisible present: I'm totally doing that again with everyone at Christmas.

MYCROFT CHRISTIE: I wish you luck. Might I enquire as to the significance of Tuesday afternoons?

HEIDI: Picnics under the cherry tree by the lake. I figure the "miss you like. . ." thing can be a running gag between us. You know, every time he posts he says something from our many happy hours together: I miss you like sharing apple pie, I miss you like holding hands in the sunset. . .

MYCROFT CHRISTIE: I miss you like correct speech and punctuation?

HEIDI: Shut it, future boy. You've got a malfunctioning Twenty-First-Century Linguistic Etiquette Implant, which makes you talk like a loon. Ed doesn't.

MYCROFT CHRISTIE: I'm not sure this young man is a good influence on you. You're getting rather cheeky.

HEIDI: Who, me? (fluttery eyelashes)

MYCROFT CHRISTIE: (smouldery eyebrow, jealous look)

HEIDI: Ahem. Yes. Do you think I should add some kisses at the end?

MYCROFT CHRISTIE: As you'll recall from the undelivered letter in episode 2.12: *The Chargé D'Affaires Affair*, my preferred sign-off is "With love & affection".

HEIDI: It's a good job you're pretty, isn't it?

MYCROFT CHRISTIE: (sighs, continues smouldery eyebrow to fade-out)

And that's it. He's done. Gingerbread Ed Hartley, fresh from the oven, and ready to serve.

ORE.

SUM.

I'm kind of desperate to show him off right away, but I have to be a professional about this. My many hours of TV detective training has taught me the importance of patience: of hanging back, and waiting for the quarry to take the bait, in case the quarry turn out to be flying manmonkeys of death. Not that I'm exactly expecting that. And Mycroft and Jori on stakeout eating doughnuts definitely get to have more fun than I do sitting in History, trying to casually steer a conversation about Henry VIII round to hot boyfriendly types. But blurting out "please go and look at this website where you will find convincing evidence of how much Ed loves me" could ruin the whole operation.

Result: I'm practically skipping when I hit the Little Leaf for my next shift, and get to at least share him with *someone*.

I dutifully strap on my frilly apron, and admire today's Wisdom: OUR BLUE POPPY SEED CAKE IS NOT ACTUALLY BLUE: *just the poppy seeds in it. Sorry to disappoint.* I sling toast, jam, English Breakfast pot for two at the ancient couple seated at the window. I wait for Betsy to get us set up with our own pot. Then I whack the Dread Pirate on to the counter, piggyback on to the Big Bean's wi-fi network from across the road, and introduce Betsy to **gingerbread_ed** in all his ULife glory.

I don't even dare hold my cup while she's reading. She's going to love him. She's going to think he's heaven on a stick.

She makes the face she makes when people ask for their tea with lemon. It's not a happy face.

"Oh, *Heidi*. It's sweet and all, but don't you think this is a little too much?"

PARD.

ON.

MOY?

"You don't think he sounds yummy? In an angsty troubadour kind of way?"

Betsy sighs, and casts her eye over the screen again.

"I guess, if you like that intense thing. He's like an independent movie Ken-doll. One of those guys who wants to read you his poetry while wearing a Che Guevara T-shirt."

"That's bad?"

I could be read poetry. I've already been read poetry. By the lake, all summer, under the cherry tree. I've just decided. I've always pictured him in a sort of geek-chic flowery shirt before now, but Ed could totally rock a Che T-shirt. In a post-political post-ironic don't-really-know-what-this-means kind of way.

"It's bad if the poetry is bad, hon. Which, let's face it, it's going to be. Have you ever actually read Jack Kerouac?"

"No. But Ed would love it. It's required reading for open-roading big-sky biker types. Like how all emogirls have to read *The Bell Jar*."

"Uh-huh."

Betsy takes a long sip of tea.

"Oh My God. You don't like my boyfriend."

Betsy squints under her fringe. "Nonono, honeybee. He's . . . cute as a button. And you're obviously enjoying yourself, making all this up. It's just he's, I don't know, maybe a little more revealing than you realize? He's not a person, after all: he's a list of things Heidi finds attractive in a guy. That's kind of personal material to be putting out there, hon. It's like I'm peeking inside your head, getting all surprised by what's going on up there."

"Surprised?" That doesn't sound good. I thought Ed was perfect and gorgeous in a universally accepted, non-Heidi-specific kind of way. "You mean, I got the list of attractive stuff wrong?"

"No, sweetie. That's not the kind of thing you can get wrong. I guess . . . well, I guess I'm just surprised you *have* a list."

"Don't let The Coat fool you, missy," I say, waving a spoon at her.

"Beneath this cunning disguise, I am actually a girl. A girly girl, who has girly thoughts about boylike boys. Bad thoughts. Bad, naughty, girly thoughts."

There's a little cough, cutting me off from my spoon-waving.

Teddy.

Edging behind Betsy and looking deliriously rumpled like always, curls askew, in a floury apron and his monster feet slippers.

"I'll just be over here, completely unable to hear you," he says, wiping down the Daily Wisdom and replacing it with WHY NOT TRY A CUP OF EARL GREY? *We have run out of milk.*

"Again?" says Betsy, twisting round to read. "Crap. Teddy, sweetie, drop round the corner store and pick up a couple of pints? Excuse me, Heidi, I have to go yell at some suppliers."

I nod vaguely, eyes already back on the keyboard. We've only got two customers, and they've been served. We're milkless. Perfect opportunity for me to do what any self-respecting girlfriend would be doing right now: chat online with my boy.

UChat

mrsheidichristie: Hey eddiebaby! You still alive or did Bilbo stink you to death?

gingerbread_ed: he stank me to death. apparently i have been reincarnated as some guy called 'eddiebaby'. :/

mrsheidichristie: Humblest apologies, edmondo.

gingerbread_ed: aren't you supposed to be at work?

mrsheidichristie: Yeah, we're not very busy though. Betsy says hi!

gingerbread_ed: give her a snog from me?

mrsheidichristie: um . . . no. I could send you an almond finger?

gingerbread_ed: mmm, kinky

I have to switch between two different browsers so I can be logged into both accounts, which is a pain. But it's worth it. It looks super-amazing. Even Betsy's impressed, when she comes back in.

"OK, I'm starting to like him," she says, reading over my shoulder once I'm safely logged back out again, my tracks covered. "You, I'm a little worried about. You're a little too good at this, you know that?"

"It's all Ed's fault. He's leading me astray."

She smiles. I think she's finally getting why this is fun. Then she peers at the screen again.

"Wait. These are private messages, right? So only you and Ed can read them? I mean, in theory."

See? She's starting to think he's real too.

"In theory, yeah."

"So if no one else can see this stuff, what's the point?"

I check my watch and grin.

Mycroft Christie, episode 2.2: *The Burmese Falcon. Contrary to popular belief, my dear, I know precisely what I'm doing.*

The Little Leaf door opens with a jingle and in walks my audience.

The Leftover Squad. Full line-up: Ludo snuggled halfway inside Peroxide Eric's military coat; Fili and Simon, the doom twins, gauntly perfect in identical black skinnies and pointy boots; Dai bouncing in like Tigger, and propelling Henry forward to show him off.

Betsy raises an eyebrow.

"Hey, guys, was wondering if you'd make it," I say, ultra-casual, gently nudging the Dread Pirate to ensure the screen is enticingly visible.

I catch Betsy's eye.

OWE.

YES.

Phase Two of Operation Authentic Boy is going perfectly to plan.

The Lovely Safak drops in to see Teddy and helps out in the kitchen between kissy-breaks. I scribble down orders, smirking as Fili and Simon murmur their matching requests for the most Goth items on the menu (blackcurrant tea and Darkest Chocolate Brownies). I worry for a minute at Henry's amused look, as he takes in the mismatched mugs and the worn bit on the arm of the sofa: he's probably used to posh china and waitresses who don't spill things on you. But Betsy threatens to force-feed Dai cream teas if he gets any more buff (which makes him go all pink, even though you can tell he's loving it), and Henry shakes her hand and they geek out together over Ceylon versus Darjeeling. Peroxide Eric sprawls on the green velvet sofa, Ludo snuggling pointedly further into his coat, one beady eye watching Safak lean over the counter to ruffle the flour out of Teddy's hair.

And I observe, invisibly, as Dai's curiosity drags him to sneak a peek at the open laptop, as he whispers gleefully to Ludo – who then quite urgently needs a teaspoon, and to linger at the counter reading while she's finding one: as the laptop catches Fili's eye too while she's waiting in the bathroom queue, and she blinks at it, while Dai and Ludo watch and giggle from the green velvet sofa.

"So, what's up?" I say innocently, hopping up on the nearest table.

Ludo, Dai and Henry exchange smirky, faintly guilty looks.

"Dai's being a crazy dumb person," says Ludo, barely missing a beat.

This is even better than I'd hoped. Now they're pretending Ed is their little secret too.

"Afraid so," says Henry, smoothly picking up the thread like a pro. "Mr Busy and Important here has decided he's too good for slumming it on the stage."

"Even though it's going to be, like, THE thing that everyone is doing and we're, like, never even going to SEE him this term if he doesn't," adds Ludo.

Dai throws up his hands. "All I said was I might not be able to do swimming *and* squash club *and* the musical. Which is apparently the end of the world."

"He thinks he did a bad audition," explains Henry fondly.

"Not true," says Fili.

"And Fili would know," Henry adds. "Secret starlet, this one. Best audition I've ever seen."

Simon beams from under his fluffy black hair. Fili shuffles a little in her seat. I try to imagine 80s-styled glittery musical superstar Fili. It's . . . weird.

"Anyway, Phil hasn't even DECIDED on the casting yet, so he should totally just wait."

"You're calling him *Phil* now?" says Peroxide Eric.

"You wouldn't understand, baby, but calling him Mr Venables is, like, SO not an accurate representation of the director/cast dynamic?"

Ludo rubs Peroxide Eric's chest reassuringly. He gives her a cute little pat on the head, and eyerolls, catching my eye as he does it. Oh yeah, Ludo's well on her way to becoming a Venablette. We're going to have to keep an eye on her.

Betsy strides up to collect a few mugs.

"Hope all these adorable couples aren't making you feel lonesome, honeypie," she says, leaning on my shoulder. "You with the long-distance relationship and all, I mean."

She gives me a huge wink. My heart does a little fandango of panic. This was not part of the plan. Phase Two is at a crucial stage: a crucial, fundamental, going-to-be-really-hard-to-explain-away-as-a-joke-now stage. Fili will mock me forever.

But Dai and Ludo are both sitting perkily upright now, like two meerkats. Henry and Peroxide Eric look sweetly intrigued. Simon and Fili have their heads bent, doing their mumblespeaking thing.

"Of course!" says Dai. "The Divine Betsy has actually *met* the Mysterious Ed."

I have no idea what my face is doing, but my throat feels like someone inserted marshmallows. Many, many marshmallows.

Betsy slaps on an even bigger grin, and tugs on one of my plaits.

"I don't know about Mysterious. Lickable, maybe? Nope: *edible*, that's the word. And, Dai sweetie, I couldn't get those two off of that sofa all summer. Could've stopped pulling sugar out on the tables, they sweetened up the place all by themselves."

Then she plumps a kiss on the side of my head, and disappears off towards the kitchen, muttering something improbable about having heard the oven timer go "ping".

Everyone is looking my way.

I prepare to explain away Gingerbread Ed's blatant fictionalness. With . . . words. Words that I will think of. Soon. Really soon.

"*Edible*," sighs Ludo into Peroxide Eric's chest.

"Betsy seal of approval," says Fili, nodding slowly, looking sort of enthralled.

"Get you, Slutgirl," says Dai. "Not that we would've expected any less. I always figured you'd be the picky type."

"I think you're embarrassing her," says Henry.

"She's remembering what she got up to on this sofa," says Dai. "The Sofa of Sex."

Ludo squeals, and claps her hands.

OHM.

EYE.

GOD.

Phase Two is apparently kind of successful. Like, a lot. Like, way more than I even hoped.

Mycroft Christie's going to dance me around the penthouse in celebration tonight, I can tell. And then Ed will probably send me a few more messages, telling me how amazing I am, and I'll send a few to him, and not even the Mothership announcing another Green Only week can possibly bring me down.

The rest of the day goes by like a blur. I'm actually confused when Betsy starts the closing-up routine of mopping, wiping and eating leftover cake. I guess that's what happens when you're in love.

"Earth calling Heidi," says Betsy, knocking on my forehead and handing me a weary-looking scone. "We interrupt this transmission to tell you to go home, in the nicest possible way."

"Sorry. I was just—"

"About to say Thank you, Betsy, for your Oscar-worthy performance today?"

I grin. She was kind of awesome.

"Thanks. If they need an understudy for the musical, I'll know who to call."

"Yeah, heard your guys talking about it. You need any time off for rehearsals and such, hon, that's OK."

"Oh, I'm not acting. Me and Fili's boyfriend are supposed to be doing costume designs. Which is kind of . . . unhappenable."

Betsy is familiar with my artistic non-skills. Even my stick men could do with improvement.

"Well, if it's sketches you need, just ask the resident artist."

She nods towards the back wall, where a summer full of 'Identify the Tourist' victims are still on display.

I wrinkle my nose without really meaning to.

"Um. Yeah. That's really kind, but. . ."

"You don't want my boy's crappy scribbles all over your fancy school work?"

That is sort of what I mean, though I hope my face doesn't show it. The *Identify the Tourist* cartoons are great for the wall of the Little Leaf but I'm not sure they'll really fly up on the hill.

She chuckles. "Hey, Teddy! Get your head out of the oven and get out here! He's actually pretty good, you know. As in, 'applying to art school' kind of good?"

"Ignore the Proud Mommy routine, please?" he says, giving me one of his easy, lazy smiles. The kind that Ed *totally* gets jealous about.

"Art school, huh?" I manage to say. "Wow. That's great. I didn't even know there were any around here."

"Won't be around here – if I get in. I'll have to do some classes for credit first, but I'm looking at a few places back in the States: maybe Chicago?"

"Whoa. That's . . . a long way away. Who's going to make Teddy's Toffee Temptation cake?"

Teddy tilts his head, the smile turning awkward.

Betsy twists her daisy rings and looks at me furtively through her fringe.

"Nothing's set, OK, hon? That's why I didn't want to say anything yet. But I guess you're entitled to know. I'm selling the Little Leaf. Maybe." She takes hold of my hand and squishes it between both of hers, though hers seem to be the ones that are shaky. "You might've noticed, we're not exactly blessed with a million customers lately. You wouldn't think it, but summer was slow this year. We're kind of going under, honeypie. And Teddy's dad says he'll pay for Teddy to go to school if it's over there, so, you know.

The timing's not so bad really. Sometimes you've just got to read the signs, go with flow, land wherever the wind wants to blow you."

I don't know what to say.

Well, I do. *Don't go. Don't leave me here. Don't spoil my perfect day. Stay here for ever and ever with your cake and your tea and your unattainably picturesque Teddy, and your being the one person I can tell anything.*

"How long?" I mumble instead.

"If it happens, we'll probably aim to be back over there for Christmas." Betsy frowns as she sees my face go all crumply. "But we'll keep you on for as long as we can, honey, I promise. And you'll always be welcome."

"I'll do those pictures for your school thing too," says Teddy, shuffling his feet.

They're trying so hard to be nice. It makes it worse somehow.

Betsy packs my scone in a paper bag, wraps me up in The Coat, and gives me a hug in the doorway before she locks up.

The bell jingles behind me, like there's something to be cheerful about.

All I want to do is hide in my room and watch *Mycroft Christie Investigates*, a really wallowy miserable one like episode 2.11: *Through the Looking Glass*, so I can have a sad cry about Jori Song's tragic childhood, and not have to contemplate my own. (Or at least hope that mine turns me into an asskicking sidekicky type with only moderate daddy issues.)

But the Mothership has made red pepper and tomato soup, and apparently I have to help her eat it.

"You'll find another job, babes," says the Mothership. "Bet that coffee place across the road will be hiring. It's always heaving in there!"

UM.

THANKS?

"I don't want to work in the Big Bean coffee shop. And it's not the job I'm upset about."

The Mothership puts on her Kind Teacher Listening face.

"I know it's a bit awkward for you, babes, not having as much money to throw around as the other kids at school. And it's nice that you care so much. But don't get yourself in a knot about it. Maybe it's for the best? Mr Prowse keeps mentioning you to me in the staff room – and not in a nice way, babes. You don't need too many distractions this year. And it is only a cafe closing down. It's not the end of the world."

I think that's half the problem. I'm quite familiar with apocalypses: if we only have twelve hours before the fabric of time collapses in on itself and sucks us into a singularity, I've got a plan all worked out. I can cope fine with the world ending; it's the world being unfair I can't manage.

After dinner I stomp up to the attic and lie on my bed. My gingerbread boy is still there, leaning nonchalantly against my desk lamp, his buttons looking especially shiny.

He's a rubbish boyfriend, Gingerbread Ed. If we were Peroxide Eric and Ludo, he'd be sweeping me into his arms, wrapping his coat around me in a big wool-scratchy hug. If we were Fili and Simon, he wouldn't even need to: he'd hug me telepathically, just by standing there holding my hand. If I was Dai, Henry would probably promise me he'd phone his dad, and move some offshore funds in to buy the Little Leaf just to cheer me up.

I suppose, sometimes, a girl just has to take care of herself.

I whack the Dread Pirate on the desk and drum my fingers, plotting. Ed's probably worried about his Heidi. We probably had a very moving conversation earlier on the phone. He's probably writing a poem about me right now, strumming his guitar, wishing he was here. . .

I log into Ed's account and wiggle my fingers over the keyboard. A text box flashes up before I've even given Ed a subject line.

UChat

ludovica_b: Hi Ed!!!!!!!!!!!!!!!!!!
ludovica_b: Just wanting to say Hi!!!!!
ludovica_b: We are all excited to meet you. :)

WOE.
UH.
It's Ludo. Ludo, talking to Ed. Ludo, talking to Ed, like Ed is real. Suddenly, me hanging out with Mycroft Christie doesn't seem quite so bonkers.

Guess Ed had better reply then?

gingerbread_ed: hey ludo
ludovica_b: OMG you are there!
ludovica_b: Hiiiiiiiii
ludovica_b: I'm Heidi's friend btw
gingerbread_ed: i know
gingerbread_ed: i mean, she told me about you
ludovica_b: OMG!!!!
gingerbread_ed: feels like i know you already
ludovica_b: haha!
ludovica_b: why are you gingerbread?

gingerbread_ed: long story
gingerbread_ed: ask heidi :)
ludovica_b: got to go bb
gingerbread_ed: say hi to eric from me
ludovica_b: OMG you know EVERYTHING!!!
gingerbread_ed: i do my best

I feel kind of giddy. And brilliant. And sick. And urgently in need of some explanation of the gingerbread thing.

Ed bought it for me as a parting gift. Got Betsy to make a special one that I could keep for ever: presented it to me in the Little Leaf, while we were snuggled up on the Sofa of Sex. The squishy eye is intentional. He's giving me a flirty little wink, just to make sure I don't forget him – as if I could. . .

I'm getting a bit too good at this, I think. And then the screen winks at me again, and I see a little envelope appear at the top of Ed's page.

Message from: **dai_fawr <dafydd.wyndavies@goldfinch.ac.uk>**

Hey dude,
Ok, so she says she didn't, but I know she messaged you – so in case you were wondering, Ludo is not actually a psycho stalker. She just comes off like that sometimes. Just in case you were thinking you were being harassed by nutters.
Don't run away screaming from Ryder because her friends resemble the clinically insane, right? Cos I think she really likes you.
Later dude
Dai (also not a psycho stalker)

The giddy feeling comes back. I know you're not supposed to want your friends to talk about you behind your back. But this is different. This is them, up on the hill, talking about me, and Ed, and how Ludo is insane, and it's giving me warm fuzzies all over.

Cos I think she really likes you, says Dai.

AW.

Message from: **gingerbread_ed <gingerbread_ed@frogmail.com>**

hey dai the notstalker,
she came off more as someone who'd fallen asleep on the ! key than the clinically insane. but thanks for the reassurance. do you do this for all your friends' boyfriends?
h likes me? that's lucky. i kinda like her too.
ed

Message from: **dai_fawr <dafydd.wyndavies@goldfinch.ac.uk>**

Hey dude,
No, I don't do this for all my friends. I just know Ludo. Don't tell Ryder I said this, but she's kind of a maneater if you know what I mean?
Later dude,
Dai, Still Not A Stalker (think my bloke would be unimpressed by that as a career move)

Message from: **gingerbread_ed <gingerbread_ed@frogmail.com>**

hey dai,
ta for the heads up. i shall try not to get eaten.
tell your henry he's got nothing to worry about: i am definitely not your

type. though h says he's very cute, maybe i should worry about her
instead . . . :)
ed

I hit refresh a few times, wondering if Dai's got any more cutely
attentive advice for my boy on how to escape Ludo's clutches
(ha!), or if Fili's going to join in the meet-and-greet, but it looks like
they're all back to being busy with their boys. Just like me.

*The penthouse. Mycroft Christie, debonair detective, is
performing the tango with his glamorous (yet intellectual)
companion, Miss Heidi Ryder.*

MYCROFT CHRISTIE: You seem rather pleased with yourself,
my dear.

HEIDI: I made a whole person, and I'm pretty sure Mr Klee told
us in Biology that it usually takes about nine months. So,
yeah. Go me!

MYCROFT CHRISTIE: Indeed. Very well done.

HEIDI: Do you have to be quite that patronizing?

MYCROFT CHRISTIE: I'm afraid it's in the script. It encourages
you to be feisty and sarcastic in return, in order for us to
reveal our unresolved sexual tension through snarky banter.

HEIDI: Oh, yeah. I have a boyfriend now though.

MYCROFT CHRISTIE: According to Season 3, I have a secret
wife from the future who's been sent back through time to kill
me. I think we must accept, my dear, that our romance is
somewhat star-crossed. I believe, however, you have more
pressing matters than those of the heart with which to
tussle?

HEIDI: Could you say that again like a normal person?

MYCROFT CHRISTIE: (sighing) You seem remarkably capable of late. Might all that enthusiasm be effectively applied to a more real-world concern? One at the bottom of a hill, perchance?

HEIDI: Ooh. You mean, save the Little Leaf?

MYCROFT CHRISTIE: Quite.

HEIDI: Because I'm so amazingly clever and brilliant?

MYCROFT CHRISTIE: And so charmingly modest, Miss Ryder.

Miss Heidi Ryder plucks a rose stem from a vase, thrusts it between Mycroft Christie's teeth, and begins to lead the dance.

Recipe for *Twelfth Night* by William Shakespeare

Ingredients:

Identical girl/boy twins (Viola and Sebastian)

Lovestruck duke Orsino

Olivia, the posh bird he fancies

Malvolio, an annoying butler

Feste, the world's most depressing clown

Swordfighting comedy lords

Drunk people

Confusing gay subtext

A big boat

Method:

- Crash big boat on an island, causing Viola (the girl twin) and Sebastian (the boy twin) to become separated and think the other is dead
- Lightly whisk Viola until she decides to dress up like a boy called Cesario
- Add Olivia, who falls in love with Cesario (which is a bit gay as he is a girl)
- Add Orsino, who also falls in love with Cesario (which isn't technically gay as he is a girl, but then Orsino doesn't know that)
- Mix remaining lords, drunks, servants and clowns into a big gloppy mess
- At last minute, throw Sebastian into the bowl

- Finish with some convenient marriages between Not Gay At All Orsino and his very female bride Viola, and Not Gay At All Olivia and her conveniently identical-to-his-sister bridegroom Sebastian
- Perform repeatedly for 400 years

Recipe for *Twelfth Night: The Musical!* by Phil Venables, with help from Mr W. S.

Ingredients:

Identical girl/boy twins (Viola and Sebastian)

Lovestruck niteclub manager Duke

Olivia, the rival bar owner he fancies

Malcolm Malvolio, pop impresario

Feste, a barfly

Stiletto-wielding podium dancers

Drunk people

Confusing gay subtext

A spaceship

Method:

- Crash spaceship into planet Earth in 1983, causing space travellers from Mars Viola (the girl twin) and Sebastian (the boy twin) to become separated and think the other is dead
- Repeat above method, substituting ingredients as appropriate, while listening to 'Tainted Love' by Soft Cell
- Perform once, hopefully at the end-of-term Wassail party

I hit the dining hall with my head full of pre-prepared answers to Ed questions and tea-related plots, but my love life and Operation

Little Leaf have to take a back seat. The *Twelfth Night: The Musical!* cast list is out.

"It's just TOTALLY unfair. I mean, there should be RULES or something." Ludo rests her chin on Peroxide Eric's shoulder. "Don't you think there should be RULES or something?"

Peroxide Eric yawns and shrugs. "I don't get the big badness. You all have parts, right? Speaking roles, singing, all of that?"

He's right. Henry is going to be Duke, the main guy. Fili is Feste, the sad clown, which is somehow the most perfect thing in the world. Ludo is Maria the niteclub cleaner: not the biggest role in the world, but she has lots of scenes with Malcolm Malvolio – and that's Dai.

"Except for those of us who didn't actually want to run around on stage wearing tinfoil, right, Heidi?" Peroxide Eric adds, giving me a little smirk.

"And Simon," murmurs Fili.

Simon raises his hand, like we're in assembly.

"It's not about who's not in it," says Dai, slumping over a plate of floppy salad. "It's about who *is*."

"It's all right for you," says Henry, nudging him. "I'm the one who's got to pretend to fall in love with her."

Peroxide Eric looks blank.

"Scheherezade Adams," supplies Fili.

"Scheh . . . she's the one with the. . .?"

"Nose job," says Ludo firmly, before Eric can actually perform his very ill-advised mime. "And HELLO, SURPRISE, she's Viola. Like, the main girl. The heroine. The best part? When she, like, TOTALLY can't even sing or anything. She just points her boobage at people and they're like, deaf and blind or something."

"On the upside, she has to dress up like a boy for most of the play," I say. "The boobage will be under wraps. Squished. They'll probably have to tape them down."

Silence.

"What?"

Henry pats me gently on the arm. "I believe we're admiring your enthusiasm."

"Hey, I think Heidi could be on to something," says Peroxide Eric, tugging on the dangly part of the piercing in his lip and grinning. "If the source of all her evil power is boobage, maybe she's like Samson, you know? Tape down the bazoinkas and she's just an ordinary tone-deaf mortal."

"Did you just say *bazoinkas*?" says Ludo, jabbing him with a finger.

"I'm still stuck on *boobage*," murmurs Simon. "Not literally," he adds, taking Fili's hand.

Dai sighs. "You get to be followed around by a lovesick model too, Henry. It's every cliché you've ever dreamed of."

Yuliya has somehow landed the role of Olivia, despite it presumably involving opening her mouth and sounds coming out.

"We could rehearse together!" says Ludo, her Yuliya fangirling undimmed by lack of actual conversation. "I could totally come up to your room, Fili, and we could, like, practise, all three of us together!"

Fili doesn't reply. Which isn't all that unusual really, but somehow Detective Heidi suspects she's not replying in a way that means "no".

Even Ludo notices.

"Well, not yet, obviously, because we haven't had the scripts yet," she says doubtfully, tucking her hair behind one ear.

Fili goes on not replying.

It's weird.

Henry gives Dai a tap on the back, rescuing the conversation. "Try not to panic, darling. If the worst comes to the worst, I can always try acting. I hear it's very popular in musical theatre."

Dai shrugs and goes on poking at his salad. Detective Heidi

notices something weird there too, though I'm not sure what. Dai can't really be jealous of Scheherezade and Yuliya, for obvious Very Gay Indeed reasons. But something's not right.

"Are you really going to make us wear tinfoil, Heidi?" says Ludo.

I glance at Simon, my companion in costuming. Well, in theory. He blinks back at me through his hair and shrugs.

"We haven't really figured out the specifics yet," I say, feeling mildly panicky. "Actually, I've kind of got something else on my mind at the moment. Not really a school thing, but. . ."

There's a horrible squawk as Dai scrapes his chair back from the table.

"Sorry. Got to hit the pool."

"Don't mind him, he hasn't had his vitamins today," Henry throws over his shoulder, hurrying out after him.

I look round, hoping someone else is going to explain Dai's mood, but Ludo and Peroxide Eric are a bit preoccupied with a random brunch-table snog. I look to Fili, expecting to exchange a quick eyeroll, but she's watching them with an odd look on her face.

"Homework," she says quietly but firmly, grabbing Simon's hand and pulling him to his feet.

I'm pretty sure she's not talking about the Poem On An Autumn Leaf kind. I just nod and smile as they leave, walking in perfect step.

Ludo and Peroxide Eric's snog gets epic, noisy, handsy. A cackle rings out across the dining hall: Etienne Gracey and his "guys", probably cracking up at goofy little Heidi playing gooseberry.

They don't bother me. I have a boyfriend after all. A very kind, thoughtful, useful one.

gingerbread_ed
Subject: nothin' good

song for my baby:
don't be blue, i'm thinking of you, thinking of us two, we could live in a
shoe, or an igloo? yeah an igloo would do, so long as i'm with you, coo
coo cachoo
bilbo says i should give up the songwriting. feh, what does he know.
think i'm nearly as blue as you about the little leaf. i can't believe betsy has
to close it down. no more gingerbread! hate hearing you so upset. sorry
i'm not there with my arms around you. to keep you warm in the igloo,
yeah? ;-)
h, miss you like you wouldn't even believe
ed

Message from: dai_fawr <dafydd.wyndavies@goldfinch.ac.uk>

Hey dude,
Whoa, the Little Leaf is closing? That sucks.
Hugs will be provided for Ryder anyways. I could do with one myself.
Later dude

Message from: gingerbread_ed <gingerbread_ed@frogmail.com>

hey dai
yeah, it's closing, unless business really picks up. maybe you guys could all
start eating insane amounts of cake or something?
surprised she didn't tell you. but i guess you're all busy with this musical
thing, right? she told me you got a big role, congrats man
ed

Message from: **dai_fawr <dafydd.wyndavies@goldfinch.ac.uk>**

Hey dude,

Big role is right: I'm the comedy fat guy, just like last year.

No insane amounts of cake for me: have to stay pretty for my pretty boy. But maybe we can come up with something: can't have Ryder getting all doomy on us, that's what Fili's for. . .

later dude

OAK.

HEY.

The Dai-mood is starting to make a little more sense. I've seen the script: Malcolm Malvolio is a big dork who thinks Olivia fancies him, and winds up dressed in fairy wings, chained on a cage-dancer's podium, trying pointlessly to impress her when she's totally out of his league. We're definitely laughing at him, not with him.

I suppose it's the kind of thing Big Dai got a bit too used to. And now he's Buff Dai, able to pull hot Henry types – and it makes no difference.

Another tiny envelope winks on to the screen, before I can hit reply.

Message from: **dai_fawr <dafydd.wyndavies@goldfinch.ac.uk>**

Hey dude,

God, I'm embarrassed now. Don't tell anyone what I just wrote, yeah? Not even Ryder? I'm not usually this pathetic, I swear.

later dude

I want to hug him then and there. I mean, I could be a touch miffed that he doesn't want to tell *me*, but maybe it's a guy thing. Ed's totally the kind of easy-to-talk-to mellow type, anyway. He'll be much better at this stuff than me.

Message from: gingerbread_ed <gingerbread_ed@frogmail.com>

hey dai
no biggie, mate. i'm good at keeping secrets.
ed

ludovica_b: hiiiiiiiiiii ed
gingerbread_ed: hey
ludovica_b: OMG me so sad
gingerbread_ed: yeah
ludovica_b: no more gingerbread :(
ludovica_b: is heidi ok?
gingerbread_ed: hard to tell
gingerbread_ed: she's pretty tough though
ludovica_b: yeh I spose
ludovica_b: we will look after her for you!!!!
gingerbread_ed: cool
gingerbread_ed: know you're busy with this play and all
ludovica_b: OMG yes!!!
ludovica_b: did she tell you?
ludovica_b: I have the best part
ludovica_b: well not the BEST part
ludovica_b: but I get to tie up Dai in chains, LOL
gingerbread_ed: sounds like eric's a lucky guy
ludovica_b: OMG!!!

I keep on waiting for Fili to drop Ed a little note too, even if it's just to mope over the loss of the ultimate Goth brownie supply and not about me at all. But there's nothing. I sit next to her in Chemistry, in French, in Prowse's stupid English class ("No, Heidi, writing someone else's poem on to a literal autumn leaf does not count: do it *again*, please"). I doodle little pictures of cupcakes and gingerbread men all over our *Martine's Day Trip to Paris* comprehension worksheet. But she just sighs, and works, and melts back into the two-headed hand-holding creature Filimon at the end of each lesson.

It's hard for Ed not to take it personally. He's a sensitive soul, after all. And Ed and Fili would be best friends, kind of.

The others make up for it though. When Saturday rolls around, the Little Leaf runs out of milk again, but for all the right reasons. It's like half the Finch passes through during the day: not just the Leftover Squad but the swimming team meeting to set up fixtures, the PAG set designers looking for inspiration, the French club demanding pastries.

I get a few funny looks as I spin round in my frilly apron, like they know they've seen me somewhere before but can't quite place the face now we're at the bottom of the hill instead of the top. But I don't care. Not when Betsy's so pink-faced with relief and happiness. Not when Teddy's lazy smile keeps spreading across his face, as he heads back into the kitchen to speed-beat another batch of fairy cakes.

"Thank you," I say, bringing another round of hot buttered crumpets out to Dai and Henry, and perching on the arm of the Sofa of Sex.

"Oh, it was all his idea," says Dai, jerking his head at Henry. "Our leading man is quite the charmer when he gets going."

Henry waves away the compliment. If that's what it was. Looking at Dai's face, I'm not so sure.

"I'm just here for the food," says Peroxide Eric, grabbing a crumpet off the plate and frowning when Ludo snatches it out of his hand before it can reach his mouth. "That was the idea anyway."

I smile, then look around at the mostly-full chairs.

"No Fili?"

"Expect she's busy with her new best friend *Yuliya*," says Ludo, biting savagely into the crumpet.

I frown. "I thought you liked Yuliya?"

Ludo mumbles something with her mouth full. The bits I can hear aren't very repeatable anyway.

I suppose I haven't seen Fili and Ludo spending any time together lately. I'd just assumed that was because of the boys, but maybe there's a bit more to it than that. Detective Heidi files it away anyway, as Betsy waves me over to fetch another pot of tea.

The last person to jingle the bell over the door, just as we're starting to clear up is The Lovely Safak. She stares around at the tables piled with empty cups, eyes bright like shiny buttons.

"Did I miss the hurricane?"

"Yeah, we've got this new policy where we make the waitress actually work for her pay packet," says Teddy.

Safak rolls her eyes and gives me a sympathetic look. "Do you want to slap him, or shall I?"

"Hey, Mom! Did you hear that Henry guy? Standing order for a weekly delivery up at the Finch: cupcakes for their play rehearsals." Teddy nods at me. "Guess we have you to thank for that too, huh?"

I blink. It's totally the kind of thing I would've thought of, if I'd thought of it. And Henry's doing it to please Dai, who's doing it because Ed told him to help me out, and I am Ed, so it is kind of down to me in the end. Sort of. I wonder if Dai knows about it. I wonder if he'd be pleased.

"Well, you know, thanks. It was sweet of you. To, you know, try to help out like that." Teddy ducks his head, suddenly looking almost shy.

"Aw, bless the little puppy," Safak says, running over to ruffle his curls. "I love it when he has to not be sarcastic. Now shimmy, boy. Movie starts in twenty minutes."

(I make a quick mental note: give Ed more ruffleable hair.)

"Yes, sir," says Teddy, mock saluting and unknotting his apron as he heads for the stairs.

"Hang on, I've got the—" I say, fumbling in my bag, but by the time I've found what I'm looking for, he's gone.

"Something for Teddy?" says Safak.

"It's my notes, for some costume designs," I say, reluctantly handing them over.

I only came up with them last night, after the Mothership and Dad Man decided to take me on a trawl through their teenage record collections. Watching those huge wobbly black discs spinning round, crackling and skipping as an *actual needle* scraped across them, was kind of horrifying. The Mothership and Dad Man are very very old, the needle seemed to say. They'll probably die soon. They'll want you to play "I Fell In Love With A Starship Trooper" at their funerals. I was mentally scarred by the time I got to writing anything down: I'm not sure my scribbles will even make sense.

"It's a school thing he was going to help me out with. I mean, if he's got time."

"Oh, he'll make time," says Betsy, coming out of the kitchen to give me a big warm hug. "Least we can do after today, honeypie."

"Just trying to keep my freebie cake supply coming," I say, peeking into the bag she presses into my hands. Cherry bakewells. She always gives me two, because she knows they're Dad Man's favourite. Today I've got three.

"See? Someone else who doesn't want you two to go," says Safak, prodding at Betsy's sleeve. "Consider me an ally," she whispers loudly to me, with a conspiratorial grin. "Let's gang up on them together."

Betsy's smiling, but she looks a little weary. "Thanks, girls. Just try not to get your hopes up, yeah?"

I shrug, but I don't really mean it. We've got Ed on our team. We can't fail.

Usual term-time service continues at the Finch. Dad Man catches Etienne Gracey climbing up the fire escape to Stables, and has to perform room searches on the emokids after someone writes "I heart MCR" in petrol across the herb garden and sets it alight at 3a.m. The Mothership leads assemblies on what to do if you find bags of puke in your room-mate's wardrobe. Jo-Jo Bemelmans gets sent home over a "medical issue" (also known as failing the random drugs testing).

And Mrs Kemble the Demon Headmistress adds an extra hour into the timetable for ITP, because Integrating Through Positivity with Mrs Ashe and her helmet hair is obviously going to fix all that.

Our group struggles through the usual moronic role-play scenarios (Henry was bullied by Jambo Colley for being Polish: *And how would you respond, Henry? Well, Mrs Ashe, I'd probably begin by saying "I'm not Polish"*) and writing a "contribution" of ten things we like about the Finch. That fills up the first hour well enough, as everyone chews the ends of their pencils and looks blank.

And then we end up out by the lake, Henry, Fili, Peroxide Eric, Yuliya, Jambo, Honey Prentiss, Brendan Wilson and me, all sitting in the cold October sunshine at the Circle of Peace. That's what Cooper always called it, anyway: this tucked-away little spot surrounded by trees, looking out over the lake. Everyone else calls it The Logs, because it's some logs.

I have a horrible moment of panic when I think she's going to pull out a guitar with a rainbow strap and make us all Sing Our Pain, but apparently we're sticking to a different one of Cooper's lesson plans.

The Secrets Box.

Brendon makes the inevitable filthy comment, while Ashe hands round paper and pencils, and explains it to the newbies who didn't play this game last year. Everyone has to write down a "secret", or a thing they're worried about, completely anonymously, and drop it into this big cardboard box, and then she reads them out so we can all offer our brilliant insights. She doesn't mention the bit where the secrets are usually fictional (*I'm failing Potions. My dæmon is a chihuahua and I'm allergic to dogs. I woke up this morning and realized I was a cockroach: is this normal?*), or less-than-complimentary (*I hate this lesson and have spent all of it thinking about shoes*), or the once-per-term guaranteed-a-laugh crowdpleaser: *Help! I'm trapped inside a cardboard box and people keep dropping bits of paper on my head!*

I end up chewing on the end of my pencil again. This is the first time I've done this when I actually have a real secret to keep: a really huge, gossip-worthy, Gingerbread Ed-shaped one – and there's no way I'm writing that down.

But I'm a detective. Ed's been good at finding a few things out, so far. Time I started pulling my weight.

I scribble down my "secret", making my handwriting look slightly less scrawly than usual just in case, then take the box from Henry on the log to my right, and pass it to Honey on my left. It makes its way round the circle to Fili, opposite me, who hands it to Eric, who hands it to Yuliya, all the way back to Ashe.

"Now, class," she says, peering at Cooper's script while holding her glasses-on-a-string away from her eyes, as if she's hoping it might get less cheesy that way. "Let's all remember how we'd like our secret to be treated, and make sure we grant everyone else's the same positive energy. Sharing is a very challenging thing to do, so let's be respectful." She opens the box and reaches in.

"*I have a crush on a teacher.*"

"Isn't that a bit unprofessional of you, miss?" says Brendan.

"Thank you, Brendan. Remember, it's not important who the secret is about, just how the person might feel."

"Horny, miss?"

"Respectful, I said, Brendan. But yes, there might be some sexual feelings involved."

SECS.

YEW.

WOOL.

That's how she says it, like it's some kind of rare medical condition. She's like a one-woman condom. No one would do it ever again if they had to listen to her talking about it first. It's probably why they hired her.

"Embarrassed?" says Honey.

We all immediately think it's Honey's secret.

"I'm just guessing, it wasn't *me*," she says, touching her cheek where it's gone pink. "Ew, disgusting."

"Afraid?" says Peroxide Eric.

He doesn't look embarrassed. Or afraid. No one thinks it's him.

I realize no one thinks it's me either. Having a boyfriend is *awesome*.

"Good. Why might someone feel afraid?"

"They might get what they want," says Peroxide Eric, when no one else speaks. "They're worried they're not as experienced as some old dude. Classic example of performance anxiety."

There's a ripple of giggles.

Mrs Ashe coughs. "Of course, no teacher in this school would allow such a thing to happen, Eric, as I'm sure you know. We who work in residential education are trained to manage such behaviour. It's inevitable that sometimes feelings of warmth and affection towards the people who take care of your needs here arise."

I remain unsold on the inevitability of Finches feeling the urge to make sexytime with Mrs Ashe. Especially as presumably that also applies to the Mothership.

Also, she's going to say "sexual" again. I can feel it.

"But if those warm feelings tip over into something *sexual*, then of course the teacher would gently explain that such a relationship really isn't appropriate."

"I thought sexual feelings were a beautiful and natural flowering of adulthood?" says Henry very slowly and deliberately in a perfect impersonation.

And anyway we know Mizz Cooper's lesson plan thinks so, because it's printed back there on her classroom wall, in pink Comic Sans.

"Well, yes," says Mrs Ashe, shuffling her laminated response cards anxiously. "Sexuality is something to embrace, to enjoy, to never feel ashamed of."

"Unless you're doing a teacher?" says Peroxide Eric.

"I think we're getting away from the, er, *supportive* aspect of the sharing experience." Mrs Ashe opens the box quickly and pulls out another slip of paper.

"I think we'll allow that one to remain a secret," she says, scrumpling it up. That'll be Brendan then. She reaches in for another, slower this time in case it bites.

"*All the time I'm with Girl A, I can't stop thinking about Girl B.*"

I scan the group. Unless certain people have unexpected announcements to make, the possibilities are pretty narrow. Brendan could be a contender (sympathies to Girl A if so) if he didn't write the other one. Could be Jambo. But only Peroxide Eric is leaning back with his arms folded across his chest, the tails of his grey coat draped neatly over his log, big strappy boots stuck out straight for balance, whistling.

He's not even trying to hide it. It's like he *wants* us to know.

Peroxide Eric's cheating on Ludo – or at least thinking about it.

I'm not an expert, but if Ed did that to me I'd be . . . well, surprised, mostly. But then I'd be angry. Or upset. Or both. If I was Ludo, I think I might be a little bit devastated.

I glance over at Fili, but she's in default gloom mode. Her face is completely blank. It's like she doesn't even care.

I glance back to Eric, and realize he's watching me again. Smiling at me, working it out maybe. Maybe just smiling.

"Goodness, what a romantically inclined lot you are," says Ashe, attempting to giggle and sounding a bit like a clubbed seal instead. "Would anyone like to share how they think this person is feeling? *Politely*, please, Brendan?"

Brendan closes his mouth.

"Well, I hope they feel dirty," says Honey. "And guilty. And that they break up with Girl A, because that's, like, mean."

If Cooper was here, we would now be validating Honey like she'd never been validated before. As it is, the flashing neon sign of Personal Issues goes ignored. (We all know she's talking about Etienne Gracey anyway. That guy gets around.)

"Yes, well, I think perhaps you could work on your empathetic skills there, Honey. But I see your point of view, certainly. It doesn't seem like a very kind way to behave."

"So that person *should* feel dirty?" says Henry. "Won't that get in the way of embracing and enjoying the sexual flowering?"

"I don't think *dirty* is quite the right word, Henry, no. But one really ought to limit the quantity of the . . . embracing."

"By how much, miss?" says Brendan.

I glance over to Peroxide Eric again, catching his eye without meaning to. He holds my gaze for a moment, still smiling, then looks away. He's got tattoos on his arms: biro ones, all the way up his right arm from his wrist. I'm just looking at his tattoos. That's why I caught his eye. He's looking at me looking at his tattoos.

"I don't think you can catch diseases from Girl B just by thinking about her, Mrs Ashe," says Henry very seriously.

"No, certainly not. But thinking can lead to all sorts of bad behaviour."

"You recommend we stop thinking?" says Fili slowly.

"No, no, obviously thinking is very important. But just try not to think so much about each other. Like that. In that way."

"Because it's dirty?" says Henry.

Mrs Ashe puts on a spectacular performance of the show I like to call "accidentally dropping the prompt cards for a distraction". Mycroft Christle does the same thing with the banknotes in the auction house scene of episode 2.3: *South by Southwest*, so I can't really fault her.

"Let's have another secret, shall we?" Ashe says, once they've been gathered up. "Now then: *All my friends seem to really like my new boyfriend, except for one. How can I change her mind?*"

My toes curl up inside my shoes.

OK, so it's sort of pathetic. But I want everyone to love Ed, and she still hasn't messaged him or even asked me about him, and it just so happens that if I find out Fili only likes people's boyfriends if they're from Dusseldorf and like wearing lederhosen on the sly, my boy might find himself with an unexpected makeover.

My eyes go to Fili before I can stop them, waiting for her to look up and nail it: see through me like the super-amazing brainy awesome beautiful friend she is, who would totally love Ed if she'd just give him the chance. But Fili's weaving the tasselly bits at the end of her black scarf together, sighing as if this secret isn't quite up to her standards. Just like with Peroxide Eric: like she doesn't care.

I'm totally failing at standard undercover detective protocol, so I clamp my lips together and perform a perfectly casual enquiring sweep of the circle. Who, me? I'm just one of the group. I'm just wondering whose this one is, like all the others.

"Next!" says Brendan.

"Now, Brendan, we're not here only to talk about *sexual* feelings. Friendships are just as important. So let's think about how this person might be feeling, hmm?"

"Lonely," says Henry.

I turn to look at him, startled. He's Henry Kim: I can't imagine he's ever been lonely. But he's looking down at the grass, and for a deranged millisecond I think this must be *his* secret, not mine.

"Scared?" says Honey. "Because, like, if her friends don't like her boyfriend, maybe really that means they don't like *her*?"

I hadn't thought of that. That wasn't the question I meant to ask.

Honey pinks up again. "Or him. Her or him. I don't know, it's not me, yeah?"

But now I'm looking at Fili, and it sort of makes sense.

ITP: Insanity Through Paranoia? Or Ickily Truthful People?

"So what might this person do, do we think, to deal with these feelings?" says Ashe, taking off her dangly specs and waving them so the chain goes twinkly in the sun.

There's a long silence.

"There's nothing they can do," murmurs Fili eventually, still plaiting the ends of her scarf, and looking, quite firmly, at the ground. "People like who they like. It's not always convenient. It's just how the world is."

UChat

gingerbread_ed: hey ludo

ludovica_b: hi bb!

gingerbread_ed: you ok?

ludovica_b: better than ok

ludovica_b: :-)

gingerbread_ed: do i even want to know?

ludovica_b: omg prolly not!!!

ludovica_b: think I'm in luv

gingerbread_ed: oh

gingerbread_ed: you still seeing that eric guy?

ludovica_b: seeing a lot of that eric guy

ludovica_b: ;-)

ludovica_b: sorry to disappoint you bb, hahaha

Message from: gingerbread_ed <gingerbread_ed@frogmail.com>

hey dai,

h told me you and your fella are being really sweet to her, so thanks, mate.

think she was feeling a bit blue about one of her friends? probably nothing really, you know what girls are like. or maybe you don't.

sorry, that was probably kind of rude.

ed

Message from: dai_fawr <dafydd.wyndavies@goldfinch.ac.uk>

Hey dude,

Was kinda rude, mate, yeah. I'm conversant with Team Vajayjay as much as the next bloke, thank you very much. Bet I even know Ryder better than you.

Anyway, she needn't worry. Fili's being a bitch to everyone, not just her.

later dude

The penthouse, at night. Dashing gentleman detective Mycroft Christie observes, while his lovely assistant Miss Heidi Ryder paces up and down, deep in thought.

MYCROFT CHRISTIE: I believe I'm supposed to do the pacing up and down deep in thought around here.

HEIDI: Shush. It's all right for you: your problems are fun, involve killer assassins from The Future, and can generally be solved in forty-two minutes. Mine are a bit more complicated.

MYCROFT CHRISTIE: I've had my share of experience in the affairs of the heart, my dear.

HEIDI: I noticed, Mr Dead Girlfriend of the Week.

MYCROFT CHRISTIE: There's no need to be personal. Not all of them died. And some of them turned out to be evil. Granted, that's not a resounding advertisement for my taste. But might my other area of expertise not be wholly irrelevant?

HEIDI: Beard-growing? Coat-wearing? Being kind of pompous?

MYCROFT CHRISTIE: I was referring to the art of detection. It seems to me that you have a case. Several, in fact.

HEIDI: Huh?

MYCROFT CHRISTIE: Case number 1: Miss Ludovica Bianchi, and her gentleman friend with the wandering eye.

HEIDI: But what am I supposed to do about that? She's really happy, I don't want to mess that up. But she should know if Peroxide Eric is being a git. Although he might not be, and then I'd have ruined all her happiness for no reason. But then if it is true and she finds out later that I knew then she'll hate me. So what's a good detective meant to do: tell Ludo? Yell at Peroxide Eric?

MYCROFT CHRISTIE: Or determine the identity of his Girl B?

HEIDI: Ooh.

MYCROFT CHRISTIE: Find the girl, find the crime – or lack thereof. If Girl B is blithely unaware of Peroxide Eric's interest, then he's done nothing more than think about her – and Ludo need never know.

HEIDI: And if Girl B turns out to be Tarty McSlutcakes who's been doing the nasty with him round the back of the gym, I'll tell Ludo, right after I've given him a kick in the jewels?

MYCROFT CHRISTIE: Your ladylike turn of phrase is charming, my dear. But yes, it appears you have the general idea. Now, case number 2: Mr Dai and Mr Henry.

HEIDI: Those two need their heads knocking together. Dai's lovely. Henry's lovely. Together they are lovely. Only Dai's gone all paranoid and psycho and thinks he's going to get dumped, which he so isn't, because Henry is far too nice for that. At least, I hope he is. Though I don't really know him all that well.

MYCROFT CHRISTIE: Perchance a detective might make further inquiries into said niceness?

HEIDI: *Perchance* I could. Some gentle interrogation of Henry, to check he's not going to turn out to be Evil Boyfriend of the Week and break ickle Dai's heart? Followed by squishing them together?

MYCROFT CHRISTIE: After your success at finding your own perfect partner, I dare not doubt your matchmaking skills, Miss Ryder. So, finally, case number 3: Fili.

HEIDI: Um. Yeah. I thought she was just a bit wrapped up in Gothboy, and too busy to talk to Ed. Or me. But now Ludo's mad at her and apparently she's talking about me behind my back. Well, according to Dai she is.

MYCROFT CHRISTIE: And why might that be?

HEIDI: I have no idea. OK, case number 3: figure out if Fili is being a bitch, why Fili is being a bitch, and fix both of them.

MYCROFT CHRISTIE: Excellent.

HEIDI: I do actually have homework to do, you know. It's all right for you: you've never had to investigate three sets of relationship shenanigans *and* create a scale model of the Manor for your GCSE art coursework.

MYCROFT CHRISTIE: Not especially surprising, when one considers that I'm a fictional construct and this conversation isn't real.

HEIDI: Don't harsh my metatextuality, man. I've got imaginary detective work to do.

Recipe for Magnificent Detective Activity

Ingredients:

1 intrepid girl detective
1 imaginary boyfriend
1 Peroxide Eric (potentially cheating)
1 Henry (evil or perfect?)
1 Fili (possible bitch)

Method:

- Put on The Coat, to create appropriate mental atmosphere
- Place girl detective in traditional surveillance role: tailing suspects, questioning witnesses etc
- Deploy imaginary boyfriend as sleeper agent
- Become heroic saviour of all Finch relationships

In theory, being the Finch's resident detective should be easy. All the major players are conveniently located within a small, mostly inescapable location. My surveillance doesn't need to take place behind a folded newspaper or wearing a funny moustache, because I'm undercover as Heidi, aka "that girl with the plaits", who will never be suspected to be the glamorous Miss Ryder, PI. Thanks to my network of informants (aka the Mothership, who has all the school timetables in her filing cabinet, and Dad Man, keeper of the keys to everywhere), I can track each of my targets' expected daytime locations down to the last minute.

EASE.

EE.

In practice, not so much. It's kind of entertaining, lurking behind pillars to eavesdrop, lingering at the end of the lesson to put my calculator away amaaaaazingly slowly, even doing the "oh look my shoelace is undone I must stop to tie it up immediately" trick (although either I'm freakishly gifted in the shoelace-tying department, or they don't come undone in real life anywhere near as often as you'd think). But it turns out that knowing that Henry's got French first thing on Wednesday morning isn't much use, when I'm over in Maths making Venn diagrams about hamster ownership. Lurking in the lunch queue, taking careful note of what kind of potatoes Peroxide Eric is having today (with masterful subtlety) doesn't actually reveal the innermost workings of his mind. And when it comes down to it, much as I like the idea of sneaking up the Manor stairs into someone's bedroom, rifling through their drawers and finding the envelope marked IMPORTANT CLUE – only to thrillingly hear someone approaching and have to hide under the bed – doing it for real is a no-go. I can't really steal Dad Man's keys. I'd sneeze. I probably can't hide under Fili's bed, because the dorm rooms have the kind with drawers in, and even if I could fit in the drawer, the drawers are probably already full of shoes and homework folders and stuff. Do real people even send each other letters any more?

Then there's the time already taken up with sitting in PAG Artistic Team meetings nodding a lot while Venables gets all sweaty about whether the stage wings should be covered in pink glitter or silver satin, failing to find words that rhyme with "autumn", concocting persuasive reasons why I can't eat the Mothership's broad bean purée, working at the Little Leaf (which has gone back to being deathly quiet again, and Betsy's still looking a little nervous every time she opens the till) – not to mention the fact that all kinds of significant detection-worthy action must be going on all evening, after I've gone home.

Even when I am up there at the top of the hill, I have to be careful not give myself away, by smiling too hopefully at Fili, or asking Dai too many questions about Henry, or watching Peroxide Eric to see if his eyes are wandering in the direction of Scheherezade and realizing Ludo's giving me funny looks.

Even Mycroft Christie would be struggling with this caseload.

Fortunately, like Mycroft Christie, I have a sidekick.

So by day, I'm Agent Ryder, slightly useless girl detective – and by night, I sit under my desk lamp, grin at the squishy eye of my gingerbread boy and set him to work. Life would be simpler if he'd get on with it all on his own, but sometimes a girl has to give her boy a little push in the right direction. He's not just there to cheer me up, now: he's a man with a mission. *It's a dangerous job*, Gingerbread Ed seems to say. *But it's all in a good cause, and if anything goes wrong, you can always eat the evidence.* I'm not completely convinced about that last bit (he's starting to look a bit dusty, after all, and he doesn't smell quite as yummy as he did before), but it's definitely more worthwhile than quadratic equations.

gingerbread_ed
Subject: fed up

hey

so, uh, yeah. life sucks. i suck. i even tried writing a new song called "everything sucks" but – guess what? it sucked.

h: miss you like singing in the rain, maybe you miss me too?

ed

OK, so I'm being a bit naughty, inventing an argument, and it's not what you'd call subtle, but hey, Ed's a boy. Boys aren't supposed to be subtle. (Besides, I bet the part where we made up was adorable. He probably sent flowers. Or chocolate. *Definitely* chocolate.)

UChat

ludovica_b: omg eeeeeeeeeeeeeeeeeeed

gingerbread_ed: hey

ludovica_b: you ok bb?

gingerbread_ed: yeah

gingerbread_ed: i was kind of blue earlier but i'm ok now

ludovica_b: what happened?

gingerbread_ed: i talked to h, we're fine now

gingerbread_ed: you know, relationship stuff

ludovica_b: lol yes

ludovica_b: know that stuff ;)

gingerbread_ed: yeah?

ludovica_b: yeah

gingerbread_ed: everything ok?

ludovica_b: yes

ludovica_b: no

ludovica_b: kind of?

gingerbread_ed: anything i can do?

ludovica_b: aww ur sweet

ludovica_b: must be nice havin a bf like u

gingerbread_ed: so she tells me :-)

ludovica_b: lol

gingerbread_ed: thought you all had nice bfs there

gingerbread_ed: h seems to like that henry guy

ludovica_b: yeah he's cool

gingerbread_ed: yeah?

ludovica_b: he has such good clothes!!!

gingerbread_ed: ok

gingerbread_ed: what about the guy who is seeing fili?

gingerbread_ed: simon?

ludovica_b: don't know

ludovica_b: don't really see fili any more

ludovica_b: think she doesn't like me :(

gingerbread_ed: oh

gingerbread_ed: why's that?

ludovica_b: omg, heidi talks lots about boys

ludovica_b: don't you get jealous?

gingerbread_ed: no

ludovica_b: haha

ludovica_b: don't believe you!

ludovica_b: I will have to keep my eye on her

ludovica_b: lol

AW.

Message from: dai_fawr <dafydd.wyndavies@goldfinch.ac.uk>

Hey dude

Ryder giving you a hard time? Lemme know if you want me to give her a
kick. And I've got a spare seat over here in the Loveless Puppies Rest Home
if ya need it.

Later dude

"You spend too much time on that computer, babes," says the Mothership, whenever she pops up to the attic. "Talking to that boyfriend of yours, are we?"

I must look horrified, because she smiles, and gives me one of her stiff little hugs.

"Parents aren't as daft as they look, you know," she says, smoothing down the tufty end of my plait. "Especially not ones who are teachers. We do hear things. And I know you're growing up: your father's always saying you should be doing more teenage things. I think it's nice. So no need to be so secretive, babes, yeah?"

Secretive is my middle name. (*Mycroft Christie*, episode 1.1. Though obviously it's Karen, really. Mine, not Mycroft Christie's. We never find out his real one, so maybe he really is called Mycroft Secretive Christie. Or Mycroft Karen Christie. He's from the future: they might go for that sort of thing.)

"So, is it anyone I might recognize?" she says quite casually, like she's not at all dying to know.

My eyes stray automatically to the desk, where Gingerbread Ed is listening to the conversation, with a very smirky cast to the squishiness of his eye.

"Maybe," I say, quite casual too.

Then I make homeworkish noises, until she gives up and goes downstairs to do something alarming with beetroots.

Gingerbread Ed: so delicious, even the Mothership can't wait to meet him.

It does add to the list of things I need to watch out for up at the Finch though. Agent Ryder's efforts at covert surveillance are rubbish enough, without looking over my shoulder to check the Mothership's not watching me watching Henry watching Dai, with a funny little smirk on her face. Or when we're coming out of French, and Ludo waits till we're right outside Dad Man's little office when he's on the day shift to start bellowing at me.

"OH MY GOD, Heidi, do you need, like, glasses? You're, like, STARING at people."

I give Dad Man a little wave as we go past, and pretend not to notice the way his head sticks out of the doorway to see who I might be staring at. Especially when his eyes widen in curious surprise, and I realize that Etienne Gracey just happens to be walking ahead of us.

But there's a line of people all streaming out of the back entrance, down past the lake, towards the auditorium.

"Where are we going, Ludo?"

"Duh. PAG meeting? It's been on the noticeboard FOR EVER? Oh my God, maybe you do need glasses."

I think I might need more than glasses. I've got a vague memory of promising to show Venables some costume designs at our next meeting: at *this* meeting? I did ask Teddy whether he'd done any of the sketches, last time I was in the Little Leaf, but he'd just shrugged and looked kind of guilty. He probably only said he'd do them because The Lovely Safak was there. He probably thinks it's just some pathetic Finchy waste of time. And I've been a bit preoccupied with important detective activity and saving the world: PAG and noticeboards haven't really been top of the list.

Somehow I don't think Detection is going to cut it as an excuse for Venables.

Ludo drags me into the Performing Arts block regardless, and pushes me over to where the rest of the Artistic Team are at work. Simon's there already, looking like a pale little twig with hair, wearing what looks suspiciously like Fili's favourite black jumper, the one with the little holes in the sleeves that you can put your thumbs through. He gives me a wispy little nod as I join him, ducking out of the path of Miyu Sugawara, who's staggering under a giant sparkly sign reading "Orsino's!" She adds it to the piles of painted backdrops and huge wooden props resting against an upright piano: martini glasses seven metres high, the world's brickiest mobile phone.

Panic status: moderate, increasing.

Maybe this could be *Twelfth Night: The Naked Musical*?

The sliding walls of the auditorium are pushed back, along with most of the seats, and the cast are all lined up against the back wall doing stretches for . . . some reason that probably makes sense if you are the theatrical type. Or Scheherezade just wants everyone to see her in a leotard, which is just as possible. Dai's doing press-ups, sweatily. I can see Yuliya, long arms in a graceful arc over her head, and Ludo behind her with her tongue trapped between her teeth, face scrunched up in concentration, trying to replicate it. Fili's sitting off to one side, reading her script and glancing up every now and then at Simon, like she's checking he's still there. It's probably the furthest apart I've seen them in weeks. It would be cute, if I didn't feel quite so awkward every time I saw her these days.

Ludo still has one arm in Yuliya-pose, but the other starts waving madly, and through the misted-up window I can see

Peroxide Eric, huddling out there in the drizzle with his coat collar flicked up, smoking a cigarette. That would be cute too, if I wasn't wondering whether his little smirk was from seeing Ludo, or thinking about Girl B. I narrow my eyes, switching back into Covert Detective Genius mode to track down the true direction of his gaze. I'm not being Covert enough, though; he's just looking at me.

Then I notice that Henry isn't even here, which might explain why Dai's looking quite so miserable (unless that's the press-ups), which gets me thinking all kinds of not-cute things.

The foyer doors bang and Venables comes flying in, his half-unbuttoned shirt going alarmingly see-through from the wet, and his usual cloud of hair sticking damply to his head. He does a pantoesque look of surprise at finding people already there.

"Sorry, guys, you know how it is, crazy schedule! So much to do! But it looks like you've got it all in hand, yeah? Great. Brilliant. Cast, I'll be right with you. Just got a little bit of business with my dear old friends over here. So. Props guys, looking good. See you found that glitter paint, Timo. Fantastic. Brilliant. Love it. Now, then: costume department?"

Simon and I exchange nervous looks. Well, I look nervous. With him it's a bit hard to tell.

The doors bang again. This time it's Henry, looking perfectly untroubled by the weather, carrying an umbrella and a huge cardboard box.

"Delivery for the Hungry Performers' Club!" he shouts, making his way over to us and bringing a tide of curious Finches behind him.

It's the order from the Little Leaf. Rehearsal cupcakes (though I can see some Squidgy Date Loaf and Yoghurt Raisin Oatbars in there too). I'd totally forgotten he'd done it. I hadn't even put it in my mental list of Ways Henry Is Not Evil, though that seems kind of absurd now, looking at him beaming as he swats people away, holding the box up over his head and promising goodies after they've worked on the opening number.

"For you," Henry adds, lifting a cardboard tube out of the box, and throwing it over to me. "Teddy said you'd left it down there by mistake?"

OO.

ER.

My hands are kind of shaky as I open up the tube and pull out a big sheaf of curled-up sheets of paper. The costume designs, has to be. I can feel Simon's breath on my arm, standing close, Venables standing with his hands on his hips, eyes wide with expectation.

I wish I had time to look them over first. This could be a total disaster. Part of me even wants them to be rubbish, so I'll know there's no way he'll be going to art school: no way he'll be heading to Chicago and taking Betsy with him.

But they're not scribbly rough cartoons like the ones in the Little Leaf. Not anything like those. They're proper designs: *Project Runway*-style swoopy figures with mutant rectangular heads and triangles for hands. I can see the ghost of my notes behind the ideas, but he's built them up, twisted them about, made them into something beautiful. The cast are split into two groups: Niteclubbers in sharp neons and silver flashes; New Visitors in flouncy pirate shirts and military jackets, all navy blues and red ribbons. There are scribbles of colour and tiny handwritten notes on the costumes for the twins, Viola and Sebastian (matching military jackets: hers powder blue, his pale pink) to show that when she's pretending to be a boy she wears a white stripe across her nose, like Adam Ant. I suspect this is the best idea anyone's ever had in the history of anything.

Then Simon tugs the Feste costume to the top, the one that will be Fili's: a pierrot, sad clown with painted tears, all very David

Bowie, somehow all very Fili at the same time. And then *that* is the best idea in the history of anything, too.

Teddy is a star. A pencil-wielding angel. A cupcake with legs. I'm going to do his washing up for him next Saturday, that's how awesome he is.

"*Ace*," says Venables, impressed to the point of almost shutting up.

He also says I'm amazingly talented, which is where I get fumbly and awkward and start trying to explain that actually that would be someone else. But then he starts going on about responding to the inherent cultural subversion of the post-punk era, exploiting the androgynous themes and how my faux-militarism is an amazing critique of Thatcherite economics. The rest of the Artistic Team start to crowd round and make cooing noises, patting me on the back. I go sort of blushy and giggly and unHeidi-like, and the chance to explain that it wasn't me at all kind of passes by.

Simon's too busy still gazing adoringly at the pierrot and her jaunty little hat to mind anyway. I feel a little stab of envy, watching him as one black fingernail traces the curve of the painted face, his lips slightly parted. No boy has ever looked at me like that.

And then she's there, at my side, stepping in as the rest of the Artistic Team go back to their glitter paint.

I wait, a little breathless, for her reaction. Fili's not going to leap around squeaking like Ludo would, obviously. But I know she's going to love it. It's impossible not to love it. And even though it wasn't actually me that drew it, she's going to hug me and give me one of those rare smiles, and Case number 3 can be forgotten about because everything's perfect.

Fili blinks. Flicks her eyes up at Simon. Flicks them back to the sketch. Flicks them to me and holds them there. No smile. Then she sighs and takes Simon's hand, walking away looking even sadder than the pierrot.

Heidi Ryder PI gets a little flashback to ITP, to gloomy Fili who doesn't like Ed. *You like who you like, that's just how it is.*

And I get a little shiver, and I realize it's not that I'm angry or hurt. It's that I miss her.

To: bloodwinetears@letterbox.com
From: gingerbread_ed@frogmail.com

dear fili,
this is probably a really weird thing to do, but heidi seems kind of upset about whatever it is that's happened between you. though i don't really know what that is. anyway she doesn't know i'm writing this, but i have her passwords in my laptop (that's how I got your email address) and i thought i'd just write and say that she seems kind of sad about it, whatever it is. and that she'd still really like to be your friend. and she misses you. i think she doesn't really know how to say it to your face, though, so i decided to send this.
hope it isn't too weird,
ed (heidi's boyfriend)

To: gingerbread_ed@frogmail.com
From: bloodwinetears@letterbox.com

Dear Ed,
I know how you must feel. I feel very strange writing to you like this too. It helps me to write things down when I'm feeling like this, shape the feelings into words, find the order in the chaos. I might not even send this message, but I feel calmer already now I'm sitting still, alone, still alone. Talking, without having to speak out loud.

The thing of it is, I'm a terrible person. I don't think Heidi would like me too much, if she really knew what I was like.

So it's a very kind gesture, you writing on her behalf, but I think I deserve to meet this darkness alone.

Fili

WOE.

UH.

I was enjoying Ed being Mr Sensitive. I hadn't really expected him to turn into my own private Secrets Box.

I've always thought Finches – even Leftover Squad Finches – had a sort of shell that I wasn't born with, that made them somehow unbreakable. But it looks like we're all equally squishy under our skin.

Even Fili: Fili The Unique, Fili the Tower, not Fili Who Does What It Says On Her Tin, Yawn, Next Please. She might look and sound like another Flick Henshall, but we kind of laugh at Flick Henshall and her Epic Emopain As Expressed Through Her Poetry/ Wristwarmers, and no one laughs at Fili.

I want to wake up the Mothership and make her drive me up the hill so I can give Fili a hug, and tell her whatever it is, I'll understand because she's my best friend in the world. But Heidi doesn't know about this stuff. It sounds like Fili doesn't want her to, either.

To: bloodwinetears@letterbox.com
From: gingerbread_ed@frogmail.com

dear fili,

i'm really glad that you wrote to me. not that i'm glad about what you wrote, obviously, because you sounded really sad, and even though obviously we've never met i wouldn't want that for you. but it sounded like maybe it helped to tell someone, and i'm happy i could be that person. heidi told me that sometimes you feel blue, but it's different hearing you describe it. like i can see it from the inside a little better now, or something.

i'm sure heidi wouldn't hate you, if you wanted to talk to her. i hope simon's being supportive and boyfriendly too? but you can always write to me if you prefer. i know what you mean about writing things down being a way of getting things out of you. so you can write to me whenever, and i won't share any of it with anyone unless you ask me to, i promise.

i hope you're feeling better, anyway.

ed

The penthouse, on a dark night. Mycroft Christie is seated at his desk, delicately sipping a cup of tea. His youthful associate, Miss Heidi Ryder, does not have any tea. She is not very pleased about that, but cannot be bothered to go all the way downstairs to make some, talk to the Mothership, stand in cold kitchen, etc.

MYCROFT CHRISTIE: So, Miss Ryder. How goes the investigation?

HEIDI: Horribly. Or brilliantly. It's a bit hard to tell. I've definitely found some stuff out.

MYCROFT CHRISTIE: Very good. Although I understand your colleague Mr Hartley has done most of the work?

HEIDI: Yes, but he is actually me. Try to keep up.

MYCROFT CHRISTIE: It is all rather confusing, you know, even for a time-traveller like myself.

HEIDI: Tell me about it. I keep forgetting which one of us is meant to know things.

MYCROFT CHRISTIE: Try keeping World War Five under wraps, my dear.

HEIDI: Four. World War Four.

MYCROFT CHRISTIE: (chokes slightly on tea) Yes. So. Progress report?

HEIDI: Case number 1: Ludo and Peroxide Eric. Have interrogated her and gathered valuable evidence. No Girl B suspects as yet. Propose further interrogation of relevant witnesses, and possibly hitting Eric on the head with something heavy.

MYCROFT CHRISTIE: Excellent. Case number 2?

HEIDI: Dai and Henry. Can confirm that Henry is *not* evil, that Dai does really like him, and that the two of them are kind of ridiculously adorable. Propose gently squishing them together, until they see it too.

MYCROFT CHRISTIE: I'm positively moved. And Case number 3?

HEIDI: Um. That's the horrible bit. She's not a bitch. She's just really sad. About . . . something.

MYCROFT CHRISTIE: Proposed course of action?

HEIDI: Feeling really guilty for thinking mean things about her? Followed by crying?

MYCROFT CHRISTIE: Or, perhaps, confrontation?

HEIDI: Definitely can't do that. She says she doesn't want me to know. I might make it worse, if she thinks she can't even talk to Ed about it. And maybe I don't want to know what the problem is. I just want it to go away. Could I borrow your Time Bureau guest pass from episode 3.9 and just go back to when we were friends?

MYCROFT CHRISTIE: I think you'll find I'm dressed in the grey pinstripe suit and have completely perfect hair, meaning I'm Mycroft Christie from somewhere in the middle of Season 2.

HEIDI: Oops. Bad fangirl. Don't grow that beard, yeah?

MYCROFT CHRISTIE: Might you, perchance, be changing the subject away from the emotionally distressing topic of Fili to something silly with which you feel more at home?

HEIDI: Yes. Which is a bit pointless, since you'll already know that.

MYCROFT CHRISTIE: It's getting confusing again. You really should stop being quite so many people. Dressing yourself up as others. Wearing a different costume. Playing a new role?

HEIDI: You're being kind of weird.

MYCROFT CHRISTIE: I'm hinting. You'll work it out in a minute.

HEIDI: Dressing up? But I'm not wearing a costume for PAG, I'm just designing them. Or pretending to, anyway. I don't even dress up for—

MYCROFT CHRISTIE: Hallowe'en?

HEIDI: Ooh.

MYCROFT CHRISTIE: Isn't that rather soon, Miss Ryder?

HEIDI: Yeah.

MYCROFT CHRISTIE: And wouldn't a certain fond-of-black-clothing person be the ideal person to ask for costuming assistance, thus offering a fine opportunity to casually drop in on said person and say hello?

HEIDI: You're a bit good, you know that?

MYCROFT CHRISTIE: Unfortunately, I do. But I have it on good authority that my overwhelming self-belief is all part of my charm.

Mycroft Christie sits back in his chair, and looks unbearably smug, if also quite snoggable. Miss Heidi Ryder takes the opportunity to stick out her tongue, and steal his teacup.

Recipe for a Spectacularly Scarilicious Hallowe'en

Ingredients:

Fili, keeper of the stripy tights
Dai, Mr Confidence
Ludo, shiny happy person
Agent Ryder: Undercover Genius
Handcuffs
Pumpkins, plastic hats, fake cobweb spray stuff etc

Method:

- Mix all ingredients in the Little Leaf cafe
- Hug till everyone is all right again

Special Agent Heidi has been working hard. Not on her World Map displaying the distribution of coffee growers versus coffee wealth, or a certain Poem, or even the costume designs for the musical, which are allegedly the talk of the staff room ("didn't even know you could draw, babes, you made me feel ever so silly"). But a cunning plan is underway, and the foundations have been laid. Henry and Ludo have both been provided with the relevant equipment, stolen from Venables' props cupboard.

All I need now is to distribute one last item, and sort out *my* outfit for Hallowe'en at the Little Leaf. Betsy might have adopted the tea and biccies, but she's still an American when it comes down to it. I've seen the photos from last year: there's going to be some serious festive decoration going on, not to mention a whole new menu. Me turning up dressed as A Schoolgirl Waitress isn't going to cut it.

Usually the Mothership heads straight home after classes on Fridays, but (uncannily, almost as if some clever person arranged it) Dai's asked for some extra swim time (which, strangely enough, Henry might have had a text suggesting he goes to watch), so I've got a window of an hour or so. I flutter my eyelashes at Dad Man, and he fake-sighs, pretending to look the other way as I sneak up the huge Manor staircase to Ludo's room.

She has a single, which is lucky for whoever might have ended up being her roomie, because the Ludo approach to decoration is insane: every inch of wall covered in photos, postcards, stickers; every mirror draped with necklaces and beads; desk and chair invisible, reachable only by excavation party with laundry basket. Tonight it looks like a small explosion may have occurred and destroyed the wardrobe. There are more clothes than I think I've ever owned in my entire life piled up on her bed. I'd assume it was for my benefit if it hadn't looked exactly the same last time I'd sneaked up here.

"So we're going for, like, American Hallowe'en, where you don't have to be all warty," she explains, holding up multiple sparkly, unHeidi-like items. "You know, you can be a slutty nurse, or a slutty cat, or a slutty . . . slut."

"Maybe I want to be warty," I say as she drapes a pink feather boa around my neck and pouts at my reflection in the mirror.

"Oh my God, Heidi, nobody *wants* to be warty. You should let go, you know? Lose the big coat, show a little skin! We could take pictures, send them to your Ed. Or you worried he'd get jealous?"

"He'd probably laugh," I say, imagining a squished icing eye crinkling up in amusement. "Besides, he likes me being . . . me."

I see her face, reflected next to mine, go still for just a moment. She's smiling, but in a sad sort of way.

PAW.

LOO.

DOUGH.

Dating someone as perfect as Ed does make it hard on everyone else, I guess.

Ludo pokes through the selection of stretchy sparkly things on the bed, which wouldn't fit me anyway, though she's much too sweet to say so.

"I don't really have anything warty," she sighs.

"Well, maybe not warty. But witchy. Traditional spooky stuff. Hey, you know who'd have that stuff? We should go and ask Fili."

The casual "I only just thought of this and haven't been planning it at all" tone doesn't quite come off, but it doesn't matter anyway: Ludo just slumps on to the pile of clothes on the bed.

"Good luck with that," she says.

I think about arguing with her, but there's not much point. I think I only wanted her to come with me so I wouldn't chicken out. Or to make sure I wouldn't be the only unwelcome one.

I head up the top flight of stairs alone anyway, and hesitate outside Fili and Yuliya's bedroom door.

Part of me hopes she won't answer, but there's a thump and the door opens.

Simon.

He's not really supposed to be upstairs in a Manor bedroom.

Then again, neither am I. And the chickeny part of me is sort of relieved. I'm here to just gently prove I'm still her friend, more than anything. It doesn't need to be a big dramatic scene, with weeping and guilty confessions.

Fili's curled up on her black bedcover, watching as Simon

shuffles back to let me in, and I mumble my explanation. It feels so odd, seeing her and knowing things I can't say. It's like episode 1.10: *Insight*, the one where Mycroft Christie can suddenly read everyone's minds and it turns out to be kind of inconvenient and upsetting. Except I don't have to wear an Ugly Magic Ring to do it.

And maybe it's Ed who's got the Ugly Magic Ring anyway, because I can't figure out her expression as she sighs and waves me towards the wardrobe, instructing me to help myself.

"You are coming tomorrow?" I say, poking through the black shirts, and the black skirts, and the . . . other black skirts. "To the Little Leaf? For lunchtime? There's this theme, for dressing up," I add, taking the wrapped-up prop out of my purple patchwork bag, and throwing it to Simon. "Everyone's doing it."

"OK," says Simon, nodding, then looking to Fili. "OK?"

Fili shrugs. "If that's what everyone's doing," she says softly.

She doesn't sound exactly pleased about it. But they'll be there, at least. And Operation Pumpkin can go ahead.

Betsy does not disappoint.

The rest of town is getting by on mouldy-looking pumpkins with a few triangles cut out of them, and the occasional five-year-old dressed as a witch (and getting some harsh fashion critique from the local emokids sitting on the war memorial). The Little Leaf, on the other hand, has transformed from a weird-looking place into . . . a slightly more defined weird-looking place. You can barely sit down for rubber spiders. All the usual cakes come with jammy bloodstains and sinister new names. Today's dunkable biscuit is a range of Unhappy Faces, with grumpy and/or scary expressions carved into them (and, thanks to a morning's giggling, individual names: My Little Dead Pony, Mr Sad One-Eye, Mouthless Pete). The Daily Wisdom reads THE ZOMBIES ARE COMING: *enjoy a cake now, before you crave naught but human flesh!*

Betsy's dressed as the Starbucks Mermaid, in shimmery green with two tails tied to her hair and a necklace made from coffee beans. Teddy is Jack Skellington, the Pumpkin King, with The Lovely Safak in a red wig and blue face-paint as his Sally. I've cheated a little bit, and gone for an ultra-Gothic take on Wednesday Addams, on account of the hair making it somehow inevitable.

The rest of the Leftover Squad aren't doing too badly either. Fili, Simon and Peroxide Eric in his big grey coat are dressed as usual, while Ludo's in a tiny sparkly number that must be freezing, but Dai and Henry have stuck to the brief exactly and are wearing matching pyjamas with arrows drawn all over them in marker pen. And each pair are wearing the required accessory: a big chunky pair of handcuffs, delivered by Agent Ryder as the central core of Operation Pumpkin. I might not know who Girl B is, why Fili's so sad or whether Dai really believes Henry likes him, but I reckon a little enforced romance might just make everything a little happier. If I could be handcuffed to my Gingerbread Ed, I'd do it in a shot.

It seems to be working so far. Dai and Henry look completely delighted to be unable to escape each other. Ludo and Peroxide Eric have theirs around their ankles, meaning they keep falling into each other's arms. Fili and Simon don't technically seem to need the help, obviously, but I'm hoping it might help Fili to *feel* less alone.

"I'm guessing you had something to do with this?" whispers Mermaid Betsy in my ear as they awkwardly troop in, tumbling on to the Sofa of Sex and its circle of armchairs.

"We're the Goldfinch Escape Committee," yells Dai, giving Betsy a wave and dragging Henry's arm along for the ride.

"On the run," adds Henry. "Don't report us to the authorities. We're never going back up that hill!"

"Not till tonight anyway," says Ludo, peeking out from under Peroxide Eric's sleeve. "You are coming, aren't you, Heidi?"

I make my "huh?" face.

"Flick Henshall got released from the clinic," says Henry. "Apparently someone thought the best way to welcome her back was to throw a party."

"It's going to be AMAZING? Like, all the Upper School are going to like, CAMP at the lake? And have a bonfire? Eric's going to spike the drinks and everything. It's going to be like, TOTALLY SPESH."

"It's a Hallowe'en party really, the Flick thing is just so the Screws won't close it down." Dai looks at me. "Sorry, no offence to your dad."

"None taken," I say, glancing over at the Bloody Bakewells and wondering how many of them I'll need to take home for bribery purposes.

"Please come? We can get ready together. I'll do your make-up. We could dress up all over again! PLEASE?"

"Seriously, please?" says Peroxide Eric, thumping his free booted foot on to the table. "Or I'm going to be deaf in one ear for life."

It's a Finch party. Ludo's going to paint my face like I'm her doll. I will witness at least three people throwing up. The Mothership will probably explode at the whole idea. But we'll all be hanging out together. It's the perfect continuation of Operation Pumpkin.

"I suppose I could drop by," I say, twirling the end of a plait. "But only if you all promise to keep the cuffs on?"

"She's very kinky behind that hairdo, isn't she," smirks Dai.

"I've noticed that," says Henry. "Good thing her boyfriend's not here, who knows what they might get up to?"

HELL.

YEAH.

Agent Ryder is definitely due a promotion: Licence to Be Awesome (and Watch Telly Whenever You Like). Girl B won't get a look in. Dai and Henry are probably about to get married. Fili still looks like she'd rather be anywhere but here, but all this happiness has to be infectious, right?

Not to everyone though. Betsy, for all her shiny green satin, is looking distinctly unfestive. She waits till everyone's gone, and the "GO AWAY" sign has been flipped, to tell me what a really smart detective would've figured out ages ago.

"I'm sorry, honeypie, really I am," she says, fiddling with her scaly tail. "Looks like we've got the lease on this place till December, but after that, we're gone. And even with all the people you've been bringing in, an extra waitress isn't really a luxury we can afford. We've got to save our pennies for the trip, so, well, I'm going to have to let you go."

"I told her to fire me instead, but apparently there's some kind of law against it," says Teddy, tapping his stick-on bony fingers on the counter, looking so genuinely sad under his face-paint it makes my stomach flip over.

I see Betsy nervously twiddling her big plastic rings, and Safak in her crazy red wig watching on, anxiously. So I do a big fake sigh, then smile and nod, and give Betsy a hug. She relaxes and smiles properly for the first time all day.

"You'd better keep coming in here till we close up, you hear?"

"Course," I say, managing to not let my voice go wobbly. "After all, I get to call him Rupert now, right? Customers' privilege?"

"Oh, I think so," grins Betsy, disappearing into the kitchen to wrap up some Two-Nosed Cindys for me.

"I didn't know your name was *Rupert*!" says Safak, gleefully nudging Teddy.

"Damn, Heidi, and I *was* about to tell you how much I was going to miss you," he sighs.

I feel myself go a bit pink. I think I might actually start to cry in a minute, which isn't at all the kind of thing Agent Ryder does.

"Hey, we're just hanging out watching some movies here tonight," says Safak. "Teddy – sorry, *Rupert* here was going to ask you if you wanted to come up and join us? Popcorn? Crappy sci-fi?"

"I think Heidi's got a party to go to up on the hill, don't you?" says Teddy a bit too quickly.

"Um. Yeah, I suppose so." I hadn't realized he was paying attention to the conversation that much. He's just trying to get rid of me anyway: Wednesday Addams isn't really supposed to sit on the sofa between Jack Skellington and his Sally. And I do have a party to go to, where they'll all be handcuffed to their beloveds, and I'll be . . . the newly unemployed dork on her own in the corner.

Betsy comes out with a ridiculously huge paper bag of leftover goodies, and I'm definitely going to cry then, so I give her another hug, shove a Miserable Ears into my mouth so I won't have to say anything, and run.

I get all my sniffling out of the way on the ride home, and once I've had a hot bath and eaten some more Unhappy Faces, Agent Ryder is back on the scene. I think I probably knew I couldn't really save the Little Leaf. Teddy really ought to go to art school, with his amazing drawings, even if it does mean after Christmas I'll have to live without a Betsy to talk to or a Teddy to look at. I can drink lots and lots of tea with them until then.

MYCROFT CHRISTIE: You're handling this very maturely, Miss Ryder.

HEIDI: I know! I'm great.

MYCROFT CHRISTIE: You'll be weeping about it in the manner of a fragile girly sort later, however, correct?

HEIDI: Shush. I'm going to a party where all of my friends are being very friendly with each other, and I'm very very happy, so ner.

I have to be a bit creative with the Mothership about quite how enormously close I am to Flick Henshall ("I'm not sure she's the kind of girl I really want you to be all that friendly with, babes") but Dad Man unexpectedly comes to my rescue and offers to drive me up the hill when he goes to start his night shift. The Mothership gets torn between Strict Teacher and Disappointed By Anti-Social Freakish Daughter modes, and gives in once I've promised to call her for a lift home before 10.30.

"No sneaking off into the dorms with that boyfriend of yours," she says, kissing me on the cheek as we're leaving. "Your father'll be keeping an eye on you."

UM.

YEAH.

I picture my gingerbread boy, waiting up there in my bedroom right under her nose, and by the time we're at the Finch I'm smiling again for real. OK, so I'm going to a party without him, but he's real enough for parental angst. I should go into business: new Saturday job as a one-girl imaginary boyfriend production line.

Dad Man peels off into his little cubbyhole, and I head on through the Manor and back out into the gardens. It's a horrible night, windy and wet, and I skid down the muddy slope towards the lake. Thumpy bassline. Nasty smell from outdoor candles.

Etienne Gracey and Scheherezade doing a vaguely slutty-looking dance around the world's least alight bonfire. There's no sign of Flick Henshall: just Timo Januscz, holding a handmade WELCOME BACK! banner, and one lonely yellow balloon.

At least I have The Coat. It might not be standard partywear, but my Wednesday get-up had jam on it. I've decided if anyone asks it's a costume, and I've come as the world's greatest time-travelling gentleman detective, who just happens to have autumn-friendly dress sense.

I head for the pavilion, where I can see a little huddle of people, and the red glow of cigarette ends. Peroxide Eric and Ludo (*both* smoking; that's new), Dai and Henry, all squashed together on one bench. Both pairs of them are still cuffed together too, which makes me grin.

"HEIDI!"

They all try to squeeze up, and I wedge my bum in between Ludo and Henry. Need to cut back on the blue poppy seed cake if I'm going to be doing this again. See? More reasons why being newly unemployed is actually great. Really, really great.

"Warm you up?" says Peroxide Eric, blowing smoke and waving a bottle of Something under my nose.

Ludo's teeth are actually chattering around her cigarette. Henry looks an unusual shade of blue. I think my toes may have fallen off.

I take a swig. It warms me up.

I get cold again.

"No Fili and Simon?" I say, squinting across the lake.

"Nope," says Ludo. "Haven't seen them since we got back."

"Lucky you," says Dai. "Looked like there was trouble in Goth paradise, know what I mean?"

"Really?" I say at the exact same time as Peroxide Eric does. He probably doesn't mean it in quite the same detect-y way as me though. But he chuckles, and we're so squashed together we all have to join in, like some freaky five-headed bench beast.

"Definitely some kind of argument," says Henry. "They were very nearly audible."

I wonder if I should go and investigate. My other cases are all neatly chained to one another, after all. Fili might be lonely.

Fili might still not want me around.

Then Flick Henshall comes sprinting down the muddy hill in nothing but her bra and pants, hotly pursued by Dad Man.

A cheer goes up from the other side of the lake.

"Oops," squeaks Ludo as the chase comes to an abrupt end.

"Oh," says Dai. "That's . . . unfortunate."

"Lucky it's so muddy you can't see anything," adds Henry. "Though she's probably not all that bothered, come to think of it."

Dad Man frogmarches her across the slippery grass, trying to cover her up a bit without actually touching her. As they walk, the rain begins to wash away the mud, revealing streaks of white skin. The laughing and clapping that rippled across the water from the watching crowd fades away: all you can hear now is the wet crackle of candle wicks spitting, and Dad Man's faint mumbling reassurances.

And a clinky, metallic noise, as a chain snaps, and the broken links tinkle on concrete.

The wedged feeling on the bench suddenly disappears, and Peroxide Eric is skidding across the grass in the flickery light, his big grey coat flapping behind him. Then he slips it off his shoulders and wraps it around Flick.

There's a roar of disapproval from the crowd as the streaks of white flesh disappear under the blanket of his coat. I can hear Dad Man thanking Eric as they head up the slope back to the Manor, out of sight. Flick Henshall's crying now. The crowd gets bored, and goes back to trying to keep the pathetic fire going.

"We would've done that," says Dai, watching them go.

"If we'd had the appropriate clothing," says Henry.

"My hero," sighs Ludo.

I look at the broken chain on the cuff around her leg, and think that there's probably a reason Ludo's not in the top set for English, with a socking great metaphor like that going unnoticed.

Could *Flick Henshall* be Girl B?

No. She's been in that clinic since the McCartney Party; he probably doesn't even know who she is.

Agent Ryder could take the opportunity for a little quiet snooping though. It's not like the party is all that gripping: people are drifting away in twos and threes, back to the houses, back to where it's warm and dry. Timo Januscz lets go of his balloon, which, not being the helium kind, just trundles along the ground until it lands on the lake. I should probably find Dad Man and see if he wants some extra coffee anyway. I really should go and check Fili's OK.

The others seem happy enough on the bench, watching the balloon floating slowly across the water like it's an artsy new channel ident, so I leave them with a little wave and make my skiddy way up the slope.

Dad Man's not in his cubby though; Peroxide Eric neither. Probably off finding someone to deal with Flick Henshall; maybe finding her some clothes.

I squelch my way down the tiled corridor, and pull one of the huge heavy front doors open. It's really raining now, hard enough that the drops are bouncing in through the doorway and splashing my feet. I wipe my face, and my hand comes away smeared with black from my not-waterproof-after-all mascara.

Jori Song stands around in dramatic torrential rainstorms all the time, and that never happens to her. Real life: rubbish compared to the telly.

Fili's upstairs, probably. I could call the Mothership for a lift, and just pop up to see how she is while I'm waiting. If she tells me to go away, at least I'll have tried.

I fumble in my pocket for my mobile, glancing up at STUART A. MCCARTNEY 1979, carved in gold on the Student of the Year board just inside the doors. His party goes down in Finch history. I suspect that future Finches will not be holding Henshall Parties to commemorate that time it rained a lot and everyone went home early.

My eyes wander across the board as I wipe more black junk off (or more likely around) my face.

And then I think my heart stops.

Actually stops.

Like a dead person.

Which is what I am.

There it is, on the Student of the Year board, carved in the wood and painted gold. There *he* is.

E.D. HARTLEY.

I pull my soaked coat halfway off and read the little nametag in the collar. *Hartley*.

Hartley, who I named Ed because it seemed to fit, somehow. Ed Hartley, my boyfriend. Ed Hartley, whose name is up on the wall of Manor, for anyone to see, at any moment.

OHM.

EYE.

GOD.

One car ride down the hill (complete with Mothership lecture on the correct application of make-up) later and I'm back in my attic, with Gingerbread Ed.

He doesn't look like a lovestruck angsty troubadour who tinkers with his motorbike, writes poetry and misses me like a shooting star over the roof of Stables. He looks like a biscuit. An old, stale, needs-to-be-thrown-away biscuit.

I have to get rid of him, now, right now.

I'll delete his ULife. Erase his imaginary existence. And eventually he'll be forgotten about, like that boy from my old school who stopped coming for about a year, until one day in assembly they told us he was dead from leukaemia, and I realized I'd been in school with him since we were tiny, but I couldn't really remember what he looked like.

Bryan Coleman, that was his name. I haven't forgotten about him after all. Crap.

And anyway, I need Ed. He's my sidekick. He's other people's sidekick too: Ludo, and Dai, and especially Fili. Ed wouldn't just abandon them: dash off a quick "you're dumped" blog to his Heidi and never reply to any of his messages again. My Ed would never be that insensitive.

My Ed.

Me, Ed.

I can't keep him. The profile, the messaging, they aren't the kind of thing you can just explain away as Dorky Heidi, messing about. It's gone too far now to be a joke. All it takes is for someone to see E.D.H. up there in the Manor, put two and two together, and I'm looking at a whole new brand of loneliness.

But I can't get rid of him either. There'll be more questions asked if he vanishes. Fili will be all on her own. I'll be all on my own.

I start up the Dread Pirate, still trying to decide. And I discover I'm already too late.

To: heidi.ryder@goldfinch.ac.uk
From: arealboy@letterbox.com

Dearest Heidi,
I've been meaning to write to you for some time, but never quite mustered the courage. I wasn't sure my attentions would be welcome. I like you, you see. I might more-than-like you. I thought perchance you might like to know that. And of course, online is your preferred method of communication, I believe?
love & affection,
E

WOE.
AH.
If I was feeling shaky before, I'm a jellyfish now. My fingers are all skiddy on the keyboard as I type.

To: arealboy@letterbox.com
From: heidi.ryder@goldfinch.ac.uk

E,
Suppose you think this is hilarious. Just go ahead and tell everyone how pathetic I am then, I don't even care any more. Thanks for taking the piss while you're doing it though, that's really cute.
H

I sit staring at my gingerbread boy, wondering exactly how someone ten centimetres high with sugar for eyes has managed to take over my life. Then my inbox winks at me again.

To: heidi.ryder@goldfinch.ac.uk
From: arealboy@letterbox.com

Dearest Heidi,

Did my message get mistranslated in the ether? I said I like you. I don't recall using the word "pathetic". Nor taking the piss, which I'm sure I'd recall. Do you talk to all your gentleman friends that way?

You consider me "cute", however. This amuses me. Perhaps this is the beginning of a beautiful friendship after all?

Oh, and rest assured: your secret (or should that be *our* secret?) is safe with me.

love & affection,

E

To: arealboy@letterbox.com
From: heidi.ryder@goldfinch.ac.uk

E,

OK, you're actually freaking me out now. You want to humiliate me, fine, can't stop you, probably deserve it. Just stop with the weird "love&affection" crap, because it's kind of creepy.

H

To: heidi.ryder@goldfinch.ac.uk
From: arealboy@letterbox.com

Dearest Heidi,

I perceive you're going to play hard to get. This shall be fun.

You disappoint me, however. I thought you wanted to play detective? You must be at least a little curious. Don't I remind you of anyone, even the merest smidgen? I've been endeavouring to be obvious for some time now, in fact. But perhaps you have a selection of possible suitors from whom to choose?

Until then, unrequited as it may be at this moment, I continue to write with

love & affection,

E

The jellyfish feeling doesn't go away. But now it's a different kind of quivery breathlessness that's making me stare at the screen, rereading and rereading.

The dimly lit penthouse Mycroft Christie, gentleman detective, is reclining on a chaise-longue, apparently relaxing after a party: his undone bow tie is draped loosely around his neck and he twirls a red rose buttonhole between his fingers. His companion, Miss Heidi Ryder, looks equally elegant and does not in any way have eyeliner on her chin.

MYCROFT CHRISTIE: Well, this has been a dramatic evening.

HEIDI: (makes goldfish face)

MYCROFT CHRISTIE: How attractive. Now wonder you've a new beau.

HEIDI: I haven't got a new beau. I haven't got an old beau! I've got . . . I don't know what I've got.

MYCROFT CHRISTIE: Then let's consider the matter in a professional capacity. What explanation could there be for the attentions of this Mysterious E?

HEIDI: OK. I see three possibilities. One: someone found out about Ed being imaginary, and wants to torture me before they tell everyone and humiliate me into a puddle.

MYCROFT CHRISTIE: A rather arcane technique, don't you think?

HEIDI: Yeah, but it makes more sense than possibility number two: the gingerbread man suddenly came to life and decided to send me freaky romantic emails.

MYCROFT CHRISTIE: Hmm. While I recall being menaced by a possessed stapler in episode 3.3: *When Office Supplies Attack*, I think we can all agree that wasn't the highlight of my televisual career. It wasn't terribly plausible when it happened to me, and I am, alas, fictional.

HEIDI: Well, I've always thought so. Unless . . .

MYCROFT CHRISTIE: Oh. Would I be possibility number three?

HEIDI: You do sound a lot like him. And there's the "love & affection" bit: you always finish your letters like that. And . . . now I've stepped over the line from fangirl to total frothing loony.

MYCROFT CHRISTIE: I suspect the existence of this conversation makes that point moot. Might I propose a fourth option? That this Mysterious E, whoever he might be, is a perfectly real person who likes you? More-than-likes you? Likes you enough to find out something of your tastes in debonair television heroes, and to borrow a few of their charms to woo you?

HEIDI: Dude, I'm fifteen. We don't do "wooing".

MYCROFT CHRISTIE: You're blushing.

HEIDI: Am not.

MYCROFT CHRISTIE: Are too. A very attractive shade of fuchsia.

HEIDI: Do you really think he likes me?

MYCROFT CHRISTIE: Yes, Miss Ryder, I believe he does. And painful as it is for me accept that I'm no longer primary in your affections, I suspect you might rather like him back.

HEIDI: But I don't even know who he is.

MYCROFT CHRISTIE: Indeed. Now, if only there were a talented girl detective in the vicinity to investigate. . .

Miss Ryder plucks the red rose from Mycroft Christie's fingertips, tucks it behind her ear, and shrugs on her long detective coat.

Recipe for A Tragic Break-Up

Ingredients:

Gingerbread Ed, soulful biker poet
Heidi, his beloved
Mysterious E, the new man in her life
A selection of long-distance relationship clichés

Method:

- Blend all ingredients
- Pour the mixture into the Internet, making sure it spreads evenly to all corners
- Bake till the face of Mysterious E is revealed, like those pieces of toast on eBay with Jesus on them

gingerbread_ed
Subject: oh well

so. . .
looks like i'm a single guy again.
h: miss you all the same, always will
ed

It's a risk, with HEIDI IS A BIG LIAR written in big gold letters on the Manor wall. But I need him around, and I reckon a few other people would miss him too if he suddenly vanished completely. So we're going to have a very mature and dignified break-up, where I am only a little bit lip-quivery and Ed is very stoic and handsome and probably writes lots of songs about our doomed romance, and I'll be very conveniently available for Mysterious E to come along and sweep me off my feet (which, love him as I do, my little gingerbread boy has never quite pulled off).

I needn't have worried about E.D. HARTLEY causing me any trouble though. The Finch seems to have plenty of other relationship gossip after Flick Henshall's party.

Message from: **dai_fawr <dafydd.wyndavies@goldfinch.ac.uk>**

Hey dude,
Is there something in the water? This is like the week of break-up hell. Fili and Simon, Ludo and Eric, now you guys. Henry better not decide he's got something to tell me. . .
Anyway, sorry mate. Who dumped who? Not that I'm going to take sides, natch.
Later dude

Message from: **gingerbread_ed <gingerbread_ed@frogmail.com>**
hey dai
wow, sounds like a lot happened after heidi left that party she told me that she'd been at. hope everyone there is ok. i guess at least she'll have company, yeah?
mutual decision.
ed

Hey dude,
Ha, totally guessed it was her who dumped you. No offence. It's just always the quiet ones who turn out to be maneaters ;)
Stay in touch, mate.
Later dude

ludovica_b: OMG
gingerbread_ed: hello to you too
ludovica_b: lol sorry
ludovica_b: am just surprised!
ludovica_b: I thought you and heidi were like forever love
gingerbread_ed: aw, thanks
ludovica_b: love sux anyway
ludovica_b: I hope you were nice when you split with her
ludovica_b: didn't like call her an ugly in front of everyone or anything cos that is mean
gingerbread_ed: no
ludovica_b: though bet you would not do that
gingerbread_ed: not really my style
gingerbread_ed: is everything ok?
ludovica_b: not really

To: bloodwinetears@letterbox.com
From: gingerbread_ed@frogmail.com

Dear Fili,
I suppose you'll probably hear this from someone else, anyway, but Heidi and I have broken up.

I wanted to let you know that I'm still here as a friend, if you want someone to talk to about anything. In case you were upset about anything, maybe.

Best wishes,

Ed

To: gingerbread_ed@frogmail.com
From: bloodwinetears@letterbox.com

Dear Ed,

You and Heidi are breaking up? I'm honestly surprised to hear that. But then love is complicated, isn't it? I thought my life would be instantly perfect if only I knew someone loved me. I miss being that naïve. But the garden of love is a thorny threshold. Even roses bite. You might have guessed: I'm not having the best time of it romantically myself. But being alone is all I deserve. Please don't feel you have to jump in and tell me I'm wrong, either: I'm not the girl you think I am, I promise you. But then who is?

Fili

To: heidi.ryder@goldfinch.ac.uk
From: arealboy@letterbox.com

Dearest Heidi,

When I mentioned the notion of "playing hard to get", it wasn't intended as encouragement. Ignoring me will not change how I feel about you: it's a familiar enough situation, after all. You pass by: I hope you'll notice me watching. You glance my way, smile, move on. You're quite the tease, did you know that?

I hope you're beginning to understand. This is not a joke, an insult, a childish prank. If I had the courage, I'd declare my more-than-liking to your face. Until circumstances allow, I shall have to be content with playing your game, with the rules you devised. Don't tell me you aren't enjoying the dance, just a little? I know I am. Perhaps that's why we're so perfectly suited?

I await your reply, as always, with

love & affection,

E

Finchworld is cloaked in grey fog and misery when I head up the hill for Monday morning death-by-Chemistry with Mrs Kretschmer. Flick Henshall's back in the clinic, which means Timo Januscz is walking around like a human black cloud. Etienne Gracey and Scheherazade have apparently split up, possibly just to blend in with the current trend for relationship trauma. And so have I, though I'm so preoccupied with "glancing" at pretty much every boy that walks past (just in case they happen to have a huge flashing arrow with "E" written on it above their heads) that I almost forget I'm supposed to be half of one of the broken-ups too.

Agent Ryder: your mission, should you choose to accept it, is to look sad and symbolically Coatless in the manner of someone who just split up with her bloke, while also looking devastatingly attractive and available should A Certain Person happen to pass by, while also remembering to be very surprised when you learn of other people's tragic relationship woes.

Fortunately, Dai takes on the job of rapidly filling me in on the latest developments in the break before Science, informing me that it's Official Be Nice To Ludo Day, and then somehow managing to turn that into "And Heidi Too" within five minutes (plus a bonus "I always thought you could do better than that Ed guy anyway" to cheer me up, which it does, in ways he's definitely not planned).

Ludo holds my hand very tightly all the way from Science to Geography, informing me that boys are SO horrible and stupid and we should like ALL be single for ever, yeah?

Henry gives me a hug at lunch, rests his chin on my head and tells me not to worry.

I keep waiting for the chance to see Fili, and break through our wall of awkwardness; have her hold my hand and say the same things to me, so I can say them to her.

But Fili doesn't show up to any classes.

She doesn't even make it to the auditorium after school, even though the full cast is meant to be passing through to start the costume fittings.

The buzz of electric guitars thrums through my feet before I even get through the door. Inside, Etienne and The Illyrians (the artists formerly known as The Shrooms) are standing on the stage in a mess of cables and amps and pedals, shouting at each other above the fuzz. Etienne Gracey is out front, muttering "one two, one two" into a mike. Counting: apparently not his strong suit.

"So the band will appear to *hover* above the stage, you see? Brilliant!" yells Venables, waving the pile of costume sketches madly at Simon. "Though of course I haven't signed it off with health and safety yet. . . Heidi! Just telling Simon here about the plans for Etienne and company. So we'll need four more costumes. Something different, just for the band. Really visual, yeah? Sure an artistic genius like you can rustle up something special. Sketches as soon as you can, need to get the Sewing Club on to it asap. OK? Brilliant."

He thrusts the pile of papers into my hands, then bounds off to deal with the cast.

I smile weakly at Simon, wondering if I'm technically supposed to know about him and Fili splitting up. He looks gutted enough: all drooping shoulders and hands lost in the sleeves of his cardigan, eyes hidden under the fluffy black hair. Then again, he always looks like that.

"Sorry about your break-up and everything," I say.

Simon performs a minuscule shrug, as Etienne Gracey and his guys start playing . . . something. (It's definitely "Tainted Love" at the start, but then seems to take a sharp left into "Jingle Bells", followed by some kind of screemo wall o' sound, which turns out to be Jules falling over the drumkit due to a mistimed scissor-kick.) I resolve to dress them in tinfoil. Or tiny humiliating loincloths. So long as Teddy doesn't mind me asking him to do four more sketches, anyway. It'll give me a good excuse to drop by the Little Leaf, I suppose.

"Have you got any ideas about costumes?" I shout to Simon, as we both shrink away from the speakers and head to the back of the hall.

Simon mini-shrugs again, eyes fixed somewhere down near my elbows.

I realize the drawing of Feste the clown is on the top of the pile: a beautiful sad pierrot, quietly weeping. Maybe a little too appropriate. I shuffle the sheets together and plonk them down under the folding seats.

The whine of feedback comes to a sudden stop as Henry yanks the plug from the wall, to a smattering of applause from the cast. They're rehearsing some fiddly dance step from the opening number, while Mrs Philips from the office runs around with her tape measure. Dai's smirking over something with Ludo (possibly Scheherezade ordering Yuliya to slouch more, so she doesn't look so much taller). I find myself grinning just watching them.

Operation Pumpkin didn't exactly work out, but Ludo looks happy, windmilling her arms and giggling as she stumbles into the wall.

A hand nudges my arm as the band starts up again, and I turn to find Henry there, looking weirdly furtive.

"Can't talk now, but can I catch you later?" He's actually whispering. Which, in the presence of The Illyrians, is not actually very helpful. "Secret thing. Nice secret. Sort of urgent. No, not urgent. But sometime this week. I'll find you."

Then he grins and heads back to where Scheherezade is waiting, hands on hips, yelling something about the impossibility of working with amateurs as Ludo twirls around and smacks into her. I give Dai a little wave, although he doesn't seem to notice.

The Illyrians produce another epic burst of feedback, which in turn produces more shrieking from Scheherezade, and I decide it's time to escape.

Outside it's not raining, but the air feels damp and the ground's all mushy. I skid my way across the grass by the lake, fag butts and broken plastic cups squashed into the mud from the party.

I'm slipping my way up the slope to cut through the Circle of Peace and find the Mothership for a lift home, when I practically fall on top of Peroxide Eric. He blends so perfectly with the gloom all around: greyish and pale and made out of yawns, just sitting on a log in his officer's coat. I haven't seen him all day; probably keeping a low profile. In fact last time I saw him he was chasing a half-naked Flick Henshall across the grass with Dad Man.

"Got your coat back then?" I say.

He looks down, rubs away some of the dried mud that's still on the sleeve, and shrugs.

I wait for him to say something, but he keeps his eyes lowered, almost as if he's too shy to look up.

"So . . . you and Ludo broke up then?"

"You heard?"

I shrug. "I've got ears."

"They hear anything else?"

He looks through me, past me, to the grey of the lake. He's nothing like the guy who sat here weeks ago in ITP, curling his lip over Girl A and Girl B. He looks nervier somehow, like a spooked horse.

Maybe Ludo yelled at him. She can be pretty terrifying when she loses it.

I ought to be on her side, I realize, all moral indignation and grrrlpower and yay sisterhood! She was the dumpee. She's my friend. All I know about Peroxide Eric is his taste in hair dye and his usage of the word "bazoinkas". And that he smokes, and knows where to get alcohol, and I kind of want his coat because mine supposedly belonged to my ex-boyfriend so I've left it at home, and now it's beginning to rain.

He flicks his eyes at me then, and I remember he asked me a question.

"I didn't hear anything else," I say.

He smiles sadly and burrows down a little in his collar.

"What? What should I have heard?"

He stays nestled in the warmth of his coat, but his eyes track back to mine. Grey eyes: grey like the lake, grey like the sky.

"Nothing, Heidi. Nothing at all."

Would Miss Ryder please come to the departure lounge? The Clue Bus is now ready to depart.

I'm starting to think I must have been missing a lot of Clue Buses lately. Standing at the wrong stop, on the wrong side of the road, with last year's timetable.

Could Mysterious E be . . . Mysterious *Eric*?

It's kind of obvious. If I was coming up with a cunning disguise so I could wind me up for a little while, I'd probably not call myself H.

But what if he *wants* to be obvious? E's pretending to be a bit of a Mycroft Christie himself, after all. He's got to give me a couple of clues to go on.

I wait for the Mothership to drive me home in a giddy daze, waiting to be swept away from my stupid plaits, from the Finch, from Heidiworld completely. I run up to the attic and read his emails again, hunting for more clues.

Until circumstances allow, I shall have to be content with playing your game, with the rules you devised.

Until circumstances allow.

Until after he's broken up with his girlfriend perhaps?

Until he knows his Girl B has broken up with her gingerbread man?

The Clue Bus is now pretty much running me over, tootling *helikesmehelikesmehelikesme* on its horn. (Clue Buses can do that. Like ice-cream vans playing "Greensleeves" all wonky.)

Peroxide Eric sits at the logs, in the cold and the rain, where I'm guaranteed to walk on my way back from the music rooms, and makes meaningful conversation of the sort I totally didn't get at the time but now seems made of purest meaning.

I definitely detect circumstances. Multiple circumstances. Circumstances coming out of *all* the orifices.

I mean, it's not exactly how I pictured Mysterious E. I haven't been thinking of Peroxide Eric in that way at all before now. He was with Ludo, I didn't really know him, I've been completely boyfriended-up for quite some time now and very happily, thank you for asking. But I suppose he is cute. I mean, he's not *Teddy*.

But I probably always thought he was cute. I like his coat. The hair and the piercings and the snarly way he smiles. He's got those stubby fingers from where he's bitten his nails down too much: I noticed it in the Little Leaf that first time he came in there, when he was twirling his lip-stud around. You don't notice fingernails of people you aren't at least curious about. Or lips.

He'll taste like cigarettes when we kiss. I'm OK with that. It's not a dealbreaker. Maybe we can discuss those patch thingies.

Maybe I'm getting a teensy bit ahead of myself.

He only just broke up with Ludo. I have Friendly Responsibilities to her.

He doesn't want to be unmasked yet. He's *enjoying the dance*. Who is Dearest Heidi to stop him doing the woo-the-girl boogaloo?

And I don't *know* know it's Peroxide Eric. I just kind of sort of definitely know it's him.

And, fortunately, I'm on excellent terms with my ex, who's pretty good at finding things out on the sly.

To: bloodwinetears@letterbox.com
From: gingerbread_ed@frogmail.com

dear fili,
sorry to hear things aren't going so well between you and that simon guy. heidi always thought of you two as the perfect couple, did you know? but i suppose things are never really the way they look from the outside. they definitely weren't with me and her. i think she's seeing someone else, now, actually.
are you feeling any better? if there's anything anyone can do, just ask.
take care,
ed

To: gingerbread_ed@frogmail.com
From: bloodwinetears@letterbox.com

Dear Ed,

I'm probably not the person to ask about Heidi's present lovelife:
seems like you know more than I do. Did she really see Simon and me
as perfect? That explains a lot. I love her (I hope she knows) but she is
awfully naive. I'm almost envious.

Sadness is my default setting: sorry. I emerge blinking into
sunlight from time to time, but there are usually clouds in my sky.
At least this time I have good reason to be dripping with self-
loathing. It doesn't make it any easier to get out of bed in the
morning, but the pure rationality brings its own strange sense of
consolation.

I hope I'm not boring you. It must get dull, all this moping.
Fili

Message from: gingerbread_ed <gingerbread_ed@frogmail.com>

hey dai

ok, so i feel like a dork for asking this, but i was wondering how h is? i know,
i know, pathetic ex-boyfriend syndrome. you don't have to reply if it seems
too weird.

ed

Message from: dai_fawr <dafydd.wyndavies@goldfinch.ac.uk>

Hey dude

No sweat, mate. I know how it is, you get used to talking to someone every
day and then suddenly they aren't there any more, right?

She's fine, anyway. Looks like she's moving on, if you know what I mean? Though I'm not exactly thrilled about the direction she's moving in. . .

Later dude

gingerbread_ed: hi honey

ludovica_b: hey

gingerbread_ed: how are you?

ludovica_b: still dumped :(

ludovica_b: you?

gingerbread_ed: same here

ludovica_b: we should make a club lol

ludovica_b: break ups suck

gingerbread_ed: i noticed that

gingerbread_ed:so how come you and eric split?

gingerbread_ed: was he seeing someone else?

ludovica_b: don't know

ludovica_b: he better not be

ludovica_b: will have to find that bitch and cut her lol

ludovica_b: hello?

gingerbread_ed: hey

gingerbread_ed: i don't know

gingerbread_ed: can't change how you feel about someone

gingerbread_ed: better not to pretend, i think

ludovica_b: I spose

gingerbread_ed: want her to be happy

gingerbread_ed: even if that's with someone else

ludovica_b: I spose

gingerbread_ed: would be nice if you could feel like that about eric

ludovica_b: yes it would

gingerbread_ed: aww, poor ludo

gingerbread_ed: you'll find someone
gingerbread_ed: someone who makes you feel special
gingerbread_ed: someone perfect
ludovica_b: :)

To: heidi.ryder@goldfinch.ac.uk
From: arealboy@letterbox.com

Dearest Heidi,
I know your schedule is terribly full, but it's a challenge to dance this
particular tango alone. Perchance you're simply so overwhelmed by my
charm that I've rendered you unable to respond? If so, I do hope it's
not permanent: the Heidi I've fallen in more-than-liking with is quite
the talker.
Not even a gingerbread crumb of fond attention for your real boy?
You're a tease indeed.
Nevertheless, you still have my
love & affection,
E

To: arealboy@letterbox.com
From: heidi.ryder@goldfinch.ac.uk

Dearest E,
OK, OK! My fond attention is all yours.
(I am *so* not a tease, btw.)
H

Mrs Ashe's Secrets Box could get filled up pretty quickly if it accepted multiple submissions.

Did Fili always think I was naive?

Did Dai never like Peroxide Eric?

Does ickle pretty Ludo actually go round cutting people?

Does this include me?

How long does the ex-boyfriend-hands-off rule apply anyway?

And have I got this whole thing totally wrong, because I totally tried to give Eric a gingerbread crumb of attention yesterday after lunch and he was the one hiding from me, and I think perhaps this is not a very secret secret now at all.

I linger in the doorway of the ITP classroom, trying to figure out what to write on my card before we embark on today's thrilling wall display construction (Things That Make Us Happy – which apparently may only include pictures that can be cut out of Mrs Ashe's prehistoric dodgy magazine collection, so there's going to be a suspicious absence of nipples, alcohol and Mycroft Christie in favour of knitted baby bootees and Great Recipes To Lower Your Cholesterol). Fili, Yuliya, Honey, Jambo, Brendan and The Ashe are flipping through the magazines, Fili using hers as a sort of face mask so she doesn't have to meet my eye.

No Eric, I notice with a little pang.

No Henry either, until he appears, breathless, coming from a lead cast PAG rehearsal, and dropping down beside me to share his own little secret.

"Finally I get you on your own," he says, dipping his head close. "Bless him for it, Dai's not an easy guy to shake off. Anyway, you know it's his birthday in December? I want to do something. A party? But I could use a hand with ideas, and you're pretty much his best friend apart from me."

Another little pang. I didn't know Dai thought that; since Ed's been on the scene, things have been a little odd between us. I hardly even see him these days. But I know one thing: Dai doesn't do birthday parties. Not since he was ten, and he ended up celebrating by being shoved in a bin and rolled down a hill till he smashed into a lamppost and cracked his skull open. It's not a story he tells very often. Not one he's told Henry either, apparently.

"Party? Not such a good idea. But he'd like you to do something, I bet. Actually he'd probably be gutted if you didn't. Just not anything too . . . birthdayish."

Henry nods slowly. "Right. So, a birthday party, without a party, or any reference to birthdays."

I nod sympathetically. "I'm sure you'll think of something."

Then Ashe bellows at us both to sit down and do the Happy Making Things, and Henry gets dragged off to sit with the guys.

Eric shows up ten minutes late, strolling in like he wants everyone to know he's just dropping by because he feels like it, but I can tell he's bluffing extra hard. The swagger's not so convincing if you keep your coat on like some kind of comfort blanket and take a seat near Mrs Ashe, where no one's going to go and join you. He keeps his eyes lowered, just darting them around occasionally like he doesn't want to risk any eye contact.

I miss his eyes. His deep, pool-like grey eyes. But he has nice eyelashes, I discover. They're long, sort of girly. But in the good way.

And I get it anyway. I'm probably doing the same thing: not quite knowing where to look. Halfway between smiling goofily and running away.

I cover up by cutting out a picture of a severely dubious-looking bloke with a handlebar moustache, and glue him enthusiastically to the paper, adding the caption SEXY FACIAL HAIR.

Even Fili smiles at that.

Mrs Ashe comes over and demands I stick another picture over the caption, which starts Henry off on an Ashe-baiting freedom-of-expression spree, followed by a lengthy debate on the sexiness of moustaches versus the sexiness of beards (conclusion: Santa Claus is one hot piece of ass). And then I find a picture of an orange teapot with purple cows on, which so genuinely Makes Me Happy I sort of have to stick it on.

We waste a little time staple-gunning the lunatic wallchart to the wall (Cooper never used to let us do that: staple-guns and Finches are an unholy combo), then we're pushing the tables back to sit on the floor in a circle to read the secrets box, because apparently Sharing is always best performed uncomfortable.

I make sure I'm sitting next to Fili, so I won't catch her eye when we get to mine. Which somehow leaves me bang opposite Eric, eyelashes and all.

OOPS?

We make short work of *My roomie is a phantom farter* (undeniably Jambo, whose roomie is Dunc The Monk, the guy you don't stand directly behind in the lunch queue) and *My cat died and they won't even let me go home and my sister says they're going to put her in a binbag* (Ashe: they're going to put your sister in a binbag? Honey: no, they're going to put Pom-Pom in a binbag; Us: you fail at being secret: Pom-Pom? Obviously this is deeply sad, no but seriously, Pom-Pom?).

Then it's *I might more-than-like you too*, and I'm suddenly very aware of my heart, sending all those red blobs spinning round my veins.

Agent Ryder looks casually out of the window, while also looking very casually at everyone else, as if curious to identify the secret-keeper, while also entirely giving herself away to the one person in the room that'll understand. Well, in theory. Actual Ryder doesn't have that many eyes.

Brendan suggests something filthy enough to distract all attention.

I take my chance. I make myself look up.

Eric's not looking at me.

But is he not looking at me in that effortful concentrated way that actually is kind of the same as looking at me?

Definitely.

Mostly definitely?

The eyelashes flutter for a moment, dusting his cheeks, then he tugs at his coatsleeves and runs his bitten-down fingers through his hair. Shuffles his feet around. Half looks up at me, then drops those lashes again. Tugs on his lip-piercing.

Definitely definitely.

Next it's *I'm frightened to sing* (duh Yuliya), one censored one that makes Ashe look like she sucked a lemon and stubbed her toe while a rat ran up her skirt, and *I wish I could blame you instead of me*, which is universally slated for being too successfully secretive.

And then?

Girl B is all I can think about.

And there's more eyelashing and ruffling and shuffling and *definitely definitely* definitely.

OHM.

EYE.

GOD.

To: arealboy@letterbox.com
From: heidi.ryder@goldfinch.ac.uk

Dearest E,

I just wanted to say that unless I'm completely confused and stupid (which I really hope I'm not) then I obviously know who it is you remind me of. But you already know that, right?

If I'd known these would be the rules then I would totally have come up with better ones.

H

To: heidi.ryder@goldfinch.ac.uk
From: arealboy@letterbox.com

Dearest Heidi,

As it happens, I rather like your rules; I've always been fond of dancing. But something tells me our respective paths may cross one another quite soon.

In the meantime, it is, as always, a delight to hear from you.

love & affection,

E

Romantic entanglement with non-biscuit people turns out to be very similar to going out with Gingerbread Ed.

I'm still juggling plenty of who-knows-what-about-who-and-why, which means I spend most of my day at the Finch ducking out of sight behind pillars and doorways, trying to remember whether I'm meant to be being sympathetic, or friendly, or not being anything at all. And back at the attic, I still seem to be spending my time making up conversations with someone who isn't there. Eric might not have a squished eye made of icing but him being A Real Boy isn't making much difference.

I do see him in real life, of course: the Finch doesn't make for avoidability. But he's always on the edges. Lingering at The Logs, chewing his fingers. Smoking outside the music rooms, when Venables just happens to have called an emergency PAG meeting. Keeping the required safe distance from Ludo; hovering attentively enough to let me know he's there.

I kind of love the way he does that.

But it means by the time we actually end up in the same space as one another, alone, I've already had seventeen conversations with him about Gingerbread Ed and how very lovable and non-weird his existence is, and the importance of coats, and whether Season 3 of *Mycroft Christie Investigates* would've been better without the Evil Wife (answer: yes). We've accidentally brushed fingertips. Held hands. Benchsnuggled. There may even have been kissing rehearsals.

And then there he is. The real thing, at the front steps of the Manor on an already-dark Friday afternoon, brooding against a pillar. Black roots starting to take over from the peroxide, slight stoop to his shoulders as if they're carrying the weight of a world or two, fingers drumming on the worn grainy stone. He glances up as I walk through the big oak doors and slam to a halt. I stand there like a dork. He stiffens against the pillar and blinks. Eyelashes.

Eyelashes.

Eyelashes.

Eyelashes.

"So . . . uh. Hi."

I just smile back. Words are not forthcoming.

"So. . ."

He shifts his arms to behind his back, as if he needs to hold the pillar to stand up or something. He's as awkward as I am. He's more awkward than I am. This is deranged.

"About this . . . stuff," he says, waving a hand then putting it back against the pillar, as if he might lose his balance and slip off the edge of the world. I wouldn't blame him; I might too. "I should . . . we should talk, maybe?"

I do the smiling thing some more. I think I fit in a nog, somewhere.

"Cool."

He squints, turning to look down the driveway. The darkness is split by bright lights as the Mothership's car rolls up to the steps. The engine whirrs; gravel crunches under the tyres. The headlights pick out his silhouette, framing him in darkness. He looks like a photograph, a poster, a still from the movie of *Eric: The Boy Who Was Suddenly Really Inarticulate But Also Sort Of Beautiful*.

I may be staring.

I should say something.

"That's my mum."

Not that.

"She has to take me home now."

Not that either.

"I won't be here all weekend. But, next week maybe? I stay late on Wednesdays. There's a musical rehearsal after classes: the Manor common room will probably be quiet. So I might be in there, watching TV, if you wanted to come and find me maybe?"

He blinks at me few times, like he's deciphering it: like he's really getting what I'm saying. He returns my hopeful little smile, and for just a moment I catch a miniature glimpse of E.

The Mothership honks her horn.

He shifts against the pillar again, resuming Peroxide Eric mode: solemn yet amused, artfully arranged.

Plus eyelashes.

It feels strange to walk into the Little Leaf as just another customer.

It feels even weirder to be in there as Heidi Ryder, soon to be girlfriended by Mysterious E. All the time me and Gingerbread Ed spent on the Sofa of Sex was made up by Betsy, after all. Me and Eric will be needing "Reserved" cards above it, with our names on. So long as we don't dance around each other for too much longer, anyway. The place is already starting to change in preparation for the big closedown: the hat collection's gone from the top shelf and the blackboard wall at the back is slowly shedding its fur of "Identify the Tourist" art.

Most things are the same though: the Daily Wisdom (THE CAKE IS A LIE *but you are encouraged to believe in the lemon shortbread*); Teddy sticking his curly head out of the kitchen to give me one of his insane, totally unaware smiles; Betsy gently but firmly telling me when she thinks I'm being a loony.

"Are you drunk?" she says, dropping a triple chocolate brownie on to a plate for me with a puff of cocoa dust.

I shelve my outstandingly clever metaphorical explanation of how Gingerbread Ed is vanilla and Mysterious E is rum, and try for something a little more straightforward.

(Maybe she's right though. Mysterious E *is* rum, and I am tipsy from just thinking about him. Love is so weird.)

She pours us both cups of tea, frowning as she listens.

"So this other guy starts emailing you, and he knows all about your Ed? I mean, *all* about Ed?"

"Yep. But it's OK, he's not going to tell. In fact . . . well, we're kind of . . . you know."

I fiddle with the end of my left plait and fidget. Apparently romance makes me act like I'm about five. My first boyfriend was a biscuit: it's not all that surprising.

Betsy informs me I'm insanely cute though, which seems more in line with my new-found boyfriendability.

"Anyone I know?"

"You might have seen him around," I say, all coy and girly.

Teddy reappears from the kitchen, leans on the counter and nicks a bit of my brownie. A good bit. A corner bit, crunchy on the outside, squidgy underneath. He even watches me while he's doing it, grinning, like he knows exactly what I'm thinking.

"I'll let you off for that on one condition," I tell him, digging in my bag for the list of costume requirements for Etienne and The Illyrians. I've decided to go for Lycra: just as embarrassing as loincloths, but without all that nudity making me look like a pervy weirdo for thinking of it.

"You think you can just stroll in here and demand I draw stuff?"

"You're stealing my job, my supply of peanut butter brownies, and my Betsy away to another country. Yes, Art School Boy, I can stroll in here and demand stuff."

The smile disappears pretty quickly. Teddy tucks the design list away with an apologetic nod and heads off to clear tables.

Betsy grabs my hand and gives it a squeeze. "I know it's hard on you, honeypie, but it's not all so terrible. We get to go back home, catch up with family. Some of us like to do that once in a while, you know."

"Absence makes the heart grow fonder?"

"Exactly!"

It's not really what I meant, but then she knows that.

"Means you'll love us even more once we're gone."

"You could kidnap me? I'd fit in a suitcase. I might not look it, but I'm quite bendy."

Betsy grins. "Sure there's nothing back here you'd miss?"

I look round at the bright colours, the mismatched mugs, the familiar swoop of Teddy's chalked handwriting on the blackboard menu, the list of teas indelibly in my head (Earl Grey, Lady Grey, Orange Pekoe, Green. . .).

Once upon a time, I might have wanted to parcel myself up and cover myself in stamps at the thought of losing this place, even just to escape Finchworld. But that was before there was an E to keep me company.

I spend the night before The Big Date getting all my clothes out of the wardrobe, attempting to make my hair do something that isn't two plaits (total failure) and ducking all efforts by the Mothership to "help". I feel a bit guilty, doing it all under the watchful eyes of my gingerbread boy. But we broke up ages ago, so it's not like I'm cheating. I bet Ed would like Eric: I do, after all. Ed and E should hang out and talk about imaginary guy things. They could invite Mycroft Christie round for poker. I'll end up one of those whiny girlfriends who is always sending "where r u?" texts in no time.

I think I might be a bit nervous. I've never actually been on a date before that didn't only happen inside my own brain.

Not that it's a date exactly; just an afternoon, drop-by-if-you-feel-like-it path-crossing in the Manor common room. We're just both happening to feel like doing the dropping-by part at the same time.

Well, almost.

He's already there when I arrive.

He's sitting on the armrest of the Garden common room sofa, like he's too wired to flop down into the cushions. One big boot rests on the edge of the coffee table, nudging the Finchtastic pseudosculpture of crunched Red Bull cans and photocopies on Sikhism. He's got his coat collar turned up again. It does things to his cheekbones. Good things. Very appealingly watchable things.

I watch from the door as his stubby fingers fiddle with the remote, jabbing it at the plasma screen as if infrared works better if you give it a push.

Some crappy gameshow plays on the plasma screen.

I should've got here earlier and set up the DVD player: set the timer so while we were talking *Mycroft Christie Investigates* could suddenly start playing, and we could have our first kiss to the opening credits, and then snuggle on the sofa to watch the rest. The very first episode, to symbolize our new beginning. Or maybe 2.13: *Chaos Theory*, for the Mycroft/Jori snog that we were waiting for all along. Or. . .

Eric looks up and sees me, and OK, I'm really not going anywhere.

"Hey." I wave.

"Hey."

"You having trouble there?"

"Yeah. Volume control."

"Probably the batteries."

"Yeah."

"It works sometimes if you take them out, and sort of warm them up with your hands."

"Really?"

"Yep. Well, that's what my dad says. Although he's probably just trying to get out of buying new batteries."

"Uh-huh."

SHUT.

UP.

"So. . ."

"Yeah."

In the multiple pre-shoot rehearsals of this scene, I'm pretty sure I gave myself a better script. Him too. I pictured him playing the whole thing in Mysterious E-speak, in fact. Although his stumbling nervous thing is kind of thrilling, all dark and suggestive. I'm just stumbly and nervous, without any subtext. He gets dramatic pauses: I'm the goof who can't remember the next line.

Heidi sucks at this.

H is going to have to take over.

I come in properly and swing my leg over the other arm of the sofa, so we're sitting like bookends. For, you know, really big books.

"So you wanted to talk?"

Oh yeah: H is all kinds of daring.

Eric shrugs. "Yeah. I figured . . . yeah. Like, you were the person I should be talking to, you know?"

"That would seem logical."

He does this sweepy eyelash thing that could stop clocks and traffic and maybe save the world.

"So . . . how's Ludo doing?" he says, fingertips softly dabbing at the rubber buttons on the remote. "If you don't mind me asking?"

I don't mind him asking. I love him asking. Gingerbread Ed was the asking type, which means the asking type is totally *my* type, and this is all destiny. Or something.

"She's OK. In the not-very-OK sense, natch. I think she really liked you. As in, *more-than-liked* you, you know?"

He doesn't smile at the reference. He just looks sad.

I kind of want to reach out and hold his hand, and for that to sort of tumble us into some kind of inevitable lying-on-top-of-one-another-oh-however-did-that-happen? thing. But this stupid bookends position (that seemed like a fabulous artistic decision at the time; we'd look awesome in widescreen) means I'm too far away for it not to involve trampling across the sofa, and probably the middle cushion would slide off halfway across like it always does, and I'd just fall on the coffee table and break it, or me.

"She'll be all right, you know. She's got lots of people looking after her."

He nods slowly. "Yeah. I still feel bad though."

"About moving on so fast?"

"I guess you could call it that," he says, and smiles.

His eyelashes rest on his cheeks when he does that. I should make him do that more often.

"I think it's like Fili says," I say, smiling myself. "You like who you like. You don't do it because it's convenient, or good timing, or appropriate. You just . . . feel it."

"Well, she'd know, right?"

He's looking right at me now. Those soulful grey eyes. Fingers still wandering over the remote, like they can't quite stop themselves. Little crease in his brow.

"I didn't think she'd go ahead and break up with Simon over it though. Or if she did, at least we'd end up together. Now it's like nobody's happy, know what I mean?"

He's still looking at me, all eyelashes, eyelashes doing their thing, me nodding, listening, listening to. . .

Wait.

Stop.

Break up with . . . *Simon*?

"Anyway, you're the kid who seems to know everything around here, right? So I figured you'd know if I've got a shot."

I don't know how I'm breathing. I feel like I've eaten the sofa instead of sat on it.

"With Fili?" I croak.

"Yeah. Because, you know, we had a good time. But I hear Etienne Gracey split up with that chick with the crazy name, so, you know, if Fili's not interested. . ."

"I . . . really . . . couldn't say."

Eric sniffs and shrugs. "That's girl-code for no, right?"

He tosses me the remote and jumps up, his coat brushing my elbow as he sweeps past.

"Tell her I'm sorry and all that. And thanks for being cool about it, yeah? Sweet."

Then he's gone, and it's just me, and the TV, and . . . that's not what I want.

SWEET.

SUITE.

AI.

LASH.

IS.

Recipe for Disaster

Ingredients:

Heidi
Reality

Method:

- Place your Heidi in the presence of other people
- Watch as she proceeds not to notice anything that's going on around her, despite thinking she's a detective
- Point and laugh at results

"If someone broke your heart, babes, you can tell me," says the Mothership, over watermelon and apple soup. "I'll give them as much detention as you want."

Motivational: not so much.

And I'm not heartbroken. I'm confused and scared, and back to spending nights sitting at my desk, staring at Gingerbread Ed, wishing real boys were also handily pocket-sized, cinnamon-scented and altogether less likely to make the whole world feel so meh.

I get sick of looking at his sarcastically squished eye after a while, so I turn him around and somehow knock him against the lamp. One arm snaps off. He looks even more sarcastic. I decide to take revenge, and nibble on his non-existent elbow.

It's like biting into a telephone. Or rocks. Or some other very hard thing, like diamonds, except for the vague taste of treacle, orange peel and spices. And dust. Lots of dust. Like a sort of grey icing made from ick.

Even my imaginary boy has gone off.

A dimly lit penthouse: so dim that it's quite impossible to see the face of dashing detective Mycroft Christie, as he converses with his plain and extraordinarily thick colleague Miss Heidi Ryder.

MYCROFT CHRISTIE: Truly, my dear, you have a gift for metaphor.

HEIDI: Least I've got a gift for something.

MYCROFT CHRISTIE: Might I detect a little wounded pride behind my reappearance? I was under the impression you didn't need me any more.

HEIDI: I thought I had an E to talk to instead. But apparently I've thought lots of stupid things lately.

MYCROFT CHRISTIE: The true identity of the peroxide-headed gentleman's "Girl B" was rather a surprise, certainly. But as that piece of the jigsaw slots into place, it does bring a few others along for the ride.

HEIDI: I suppose. I get why Fili was being quite so down on herself now. And why she didn't want to talk to Ludo. Or me, in case I got all judgey about her stealing Ludo's bloke.

MYCROFT CHRISTIE: And would you have "got all judgey"?

HEIDI: Um. Maybe? Just a little tiny bit?

MYCROFT CHRISTIE: Despite "you like who you like", and wanting people to move on and be happy, and – forgive me for mentioning it – rather wanting Eric all to yourself?

HEIDI: Temporary insanity. Finch flu. I'm over him.

MYCROFT CHRISTIE: Even the eyelashes?

HEIDI: I hate eyelashes. Eyelashes are horrible. From now on,

I'm only ever going out with people who don't have eyelashes. Scratch that: I'm never going out with anyone ever.

MYCROFT CHRISTIE: But what of Mysterious E?

HEIDI: Mysterious E can stay mysterious. I. Don't. Care.

To: arealboy@letterbox.com
From: heidi.ryder@goldfinch.ac.uk

E,
This has been all sorts of amusing, but I'm done. Romance is for people who are better at life than I am. Go and wave your lovely affectionate bits at someone else, OK?
H

To: heidi.ryder@goldfinch.ac.uk
From: arealboy@letterbox.com

Dearest Heidi,
Shush.
With enduring
Love & Affection,
E

To: arealboy@letterbox.com
From: heidi.ryder@goldfinch.ac.uk

E,
Seriously. It's too tiring and embarrassing and I'm way too pathetic for this to be worth the effort.
H

To: heidi.ryder@goldfinch.ac.uk
From: arealboy@letterbox.com

Dearest H,
You're flirting again.
My ever increasing
Love & Affection,
E

To: arealboy@letterbox.com
From: heidi.ryder@goldfinch.ac.uk

E,
Am not.
H

To: heidi.ryder@goldfinch.ac.uk
From: arealboy@letterbox.com

Dearest H,
Are too.
L & A,
E

To: arealboy@letterbox.com
From: heidi.ryder@goldfinch.ac.uk

E,
D2?
H

To: heidi.ryder@goldfinch.ac.uk
From: arealboy@letterbox.com

Dearest H,
It was your way with words that first attracted me, I believe.
My
Glove & Affliction,
E

To: arealboy@letterbox.com
From: heidi.ryder@goldfinch.ac.uk

E,
:P
H

MYCROFT CHRISTIE: I do believe, you're smiling, Miss
    Ryder.
HEIDI: I might be. Just a little bit. Though I still don't know who
    he is.
MYCROFT CHRISTIE: Isn't that half the fun? Now, to work, my
    dear: the game is afoot!
HEIDI: Um. Yes. Whatever that means.

To: bloodwinetears@letterbox.com
From: gingerbread_ed@frogmail.com

Dear Fili,
How are things? Are you feeling any more cheerful at all? Just

wondering, really, if you're ok. I know what it's like to be rejected, and not have anyone you can tell.
Best wishes,
Ed

To: gingerbread_ed@frogmail.com
From: bloodwinetears@letterbox.com

Dear Ed,
It's kind of you to still write: you must be the most attentive ex-boyfriend ever. If only I could inspire the same degree of dedication. I'm unworthy of it, though. Poison kisses and betrayals is all anyone can expect from me, alas.
Does that answer your question?
Fili

Message from: **gingerbread_ed <gingerbread_ed@frogmail.com>**

hey
how are you doing, man? h called me tonight: sounds like you were right, she's definitely into someone else. guess that's the way it goes.
ed

Message from: **dai_fawr <dafydd.wyndavies@goldfinch.ac.uk>**

Hey dude,
Oh yeah, Ryder's after someone else. Don't know she's going to get him, though. ;)
Later dude

gingerbread_ed: hey

ludovica_b: hi bb!!!

ludovica_b: missed you

gingerbread_ed: been busy

gingerbread_ed: but thanks

ludovica_b: did you miss me too?

gingerbread_ed: of course

gingerbread_ed: how is heidi?

ludovica_b: think she is over you, bb

gingerbread_ed: she seeing someone else?

ludovica_b: mmmmaybe

ludovica_b: ;)

gingerbread_ed: that's ok, i kind of knew

ludovica_b: you have a new gf now?

gingerbread_ed: nope

ludovica_b: thought all the good ones were taken!!

gingerbread_ed: maybe i'm not such a good one

ludovica_b: bad boy ed?

ludovica_b: lol

ludovica_b: I must be just your type

"So you've gone from dating a cookie to dating the invisible man?"

Christmas has come early to the Little Leaf, since they'll be missing the real thing. Betsy's rocking a Santa hat and shiny wrapped-present earrings, and the menu is crammed with snowman meringues and, inevitably, gingerbread men.

"Dressed like that, you don't get to mock me. Anyway, we're talking, not dating. On account of me not actually knowing who he is. Still."

I have explained the traumatic Peroxide Eric non-date to Betsy. Well, kind of. There may have been some editing in post-production.

"So why don't you just ask him?"

I shake my head firmly. "Against the rules. The whole point is he's this mysterious guy, waiting in the wings for me to unmask him. And he thinks I'm this amazing brainiac who can figure it out."

"Well, that confirms it," shouts Teddy from the kitchen. "He's a crazy person."

"Great pep talk, thank you."

"You're welcome!"

"Wait up, honeybee, I need to get this straight. There are two guys: this Eric guy you thought was all pretty and kissable, and this Mystery guy who writes you saying he thinks *you're* all pretty and kissable. And when you thought they were the same person, that was all roses, but now they aren't . . . did pretty and kissable Eric suddenly get hideous and disgusting?"

I picture Eric in my head. Eric with his long swishy coat, and his boots, and his eyelashes.

The coat is actually sort of ridiculous and smells like wet dog when it rains. His fingers are yellow. Ludo says he picks his nose. Even the eyelashes do their cheek-sweeping thing a bit too perfectly on cue to be accidental.

And then there's the added complication of his love life being even more entangled and weird than mine. There are some things I can't tell, not even to Betsy.

"It's . . . complicated. But he's irrelevant, anyway. He's 100% disinterested in me."

"U-*huh*. But does that mean you just stop liking him, snap?"

I shrug. Apparently, it kind of does. Unless I'm doing it wrong.

I could be doing it wrong.

"What I'm getting at is . . . you don't have to just say yes to the first guy who says he's interested. You're supposed to choose a boyfriend because you like him too, you know?"

"I *do* like him."

Unless I'm doing it wrong.

I'm coiling one plait around my finger, thinking about Love & Affection, while Teddy and Betsy try not to crack up.

I'm not doing it wrong.

"All this without even knowing what he looks like? Boy must have some typing skills." She tilts her head so the bell on her hat gives a little tinkle, then turns serious. "Just be careful, honeybee, OK? Don't want you getting your feelings hurt. Or Mystery Boy's either."

I nog. I've already had my feelings hurt. I'm practically a veteran at this whole dating thing. And I've got no intention of making the same mistake, and getting distracted by a Mysterious Someone Who Isn't E.

There's another tinkly noise, but this one's from the bell on the Little Leaf door.

It's Simon. He still looks like he's got a piece missing, his hand dangling on the end of his arm without anyone to hold it. He gives me a vague watery smile from under his hair anyway. I give him the same one back again, wondering if he knows about Eric and Fili; deciding not to be the person to tell him if he doesn't.

"Hey, Simon! What can I get you, honey?"

Simon climbs on to the stool next to mine and taps a black-painted fingernail on the counter, thinking.

"Banana bread?" he says hopefully.

Betsy sucks in a breath, swinging her earrings as she shakes her head.

"Heidi doesn't believe in banana in cake," Teddy explains as he brings out a slice. "It's like her religion."

This is true. Bananas in fruit form are perfectly acceptable. In cake they result in mushiness and a lingering after-taste of ming. They are the anti-peanut butter: guaranteed to deyummify anything.

Simon gives me an apologetic look, a smudge of eyeliner just visible through his wispy hair, and fishes in his pocket.

"Maybe take out the order for the Banana Blondies then?" he says, sliding an envelope across the counter to Betsy.

She grins as she takes it. "You're the boss. But don't blame me if all those Finch parents start complaining." She catches my blank look, and waves the envelope at me. "You didn't know? It's going to be the Little Leaf's last hurrah: catering for your big musical extravaganza. Guess those rehearsal cupcakes went down pretty well, huh?"

I stare at Simon as he prods the edge of his banana bread with a fork.

"You organized this? Wow, Simon, that's really. . ."

I want to say unexpected, but it seems kind of rude.

"Are these the new designs?" he says softly, reaching across me to pick up a rolled-up sheaf of paper.

Teddy must have slipped it there next to me, along with the banana bread.

The designs for Etienne and The Illyrians are just as detailed as the last lot: same swooping style for hands and faces, same little handwritten notes and scribbles of colour. And again, he's taken one little suggestion I made, and transformed it into something amazing. No ribbons or silver flashes this time: it's all skinny Lycra bodysuits with bright neon piping in odd geometric squiggles like the inside of circuits.

"Cool," murmurs Simon, his finger tracing around the neon-pink lines.

"It's all based on this film *Tron*," I explain, editing out the part where I thought putting Etienne Gracey and co. in leotards would be kind of hilarious. "These people get trapped inside a computer game, and they have to ride bikes and play frisbee to save the universe. It's . . . less ridiculous than it sounds."

"Though not by a whole lot," says Teddy, reappearing to prop himself on his elbows behind the counter.

I catch his eye, and mouth a quick "thank you". He grins, then gives Simon a sideways look, his eyes following Simon's fingertip.

Simon did that before, I remember, with Fili's costume picture. I remember thinking how romantic it seemed. Only now he's doing it to Etienne Gracey's costume, which is . . . also unexpected.

Is there some other non-Eric-shaped reason for Simon and Fili breaking up when they did? Like, Simon suddenly recognizing his inner gay?

He forks in another minute mouthful of banana cake and gives me another of those watery, apologetic smiles.

WEIGH.

TUP.

Maybe it's not the person who's going to be wearing the costume he likes.

Maybe it's the person who drew the costume. Or the person who he *thinks* drew it, anyway.

Simon, who quietly arranges for the Little Leaf to come to *Twelfth Night*.

Simon, who broke up with Fili the same night that Mysterious E first emailed.

Simon, aka Mysterious E?

UM.

WOO?

The penthouse. Mycroft Christie is wearing a fluffy black wig, and eating a stinky banana cake.

MYCROFT CHRISTIE: What? You don't like my makeover?

HEIDI: Downgrade. Sorry.

MYCROFT CHRISTIE: (tossing the wig aside, and revealing his curls) I confess I agree. But still, one mustn't judge by appearances.

HEIDI: You mean, I'm fugly and a weirdo and I should take what I can get?

MYCROFT CHRISTIE: On the contrary: Mysterious E's appeal is not too dissimilar to my own, surely? Granted, this "Simon" person lacks certain of my debonair charms, but I fancy my intellect alone makes me quite the catch.

HEIDI: You also fight crime, can travel in time and have saved the city of London from evil giant centipedes. Even if that episode was a bit crap. And you haven't recently broken up with one of my mates, who is already really miserable, for complicated reasons which I probably can't even tell you about.

MYCROFT CHRISTIE: You do have intimidatingly high standards for your gentleman friends, Miss Ryder. Besides, I believe your intention – this time – was to ascertain the identity of your mysterious suitor, before any awkward encounters on sofas could ensue. Might I propose a little further investigation?

Agent Ryder is starting to feel overwhelmed by the pressures of undercover life at the Finch. Pre-Christmas cheer is beginning to creep throughout the school, thanks mostly to Dad Man being bored and "Wassail" decorations being harder to find; tinsel round the noticeboards, a tree as tall as the Manor on the front steps, speckled with white and blue lights. But behind all the fake snow and baubles in every classroom, every corridor, there seems to be a lurking secret, a little subtext, a dangerous casual slip that could bring it all tumbling down.

Eric loiters outside the music rooms while PAG rehearsals go on, waiting for Scheherezade to come out – while Ludo watches him from inside, her chin firmly up as she twirls to show what he's missing. Fili watches her twirl, her face downcast, till she sees me looking and ducks her head – while I remember that even Ed doesn't know why she might be looking so guilty, and I turn away to find Dai watching me closely, just as Ed asked him to, while Henry lingers off to one side, waiting for him to move on so he can slide in and share some not-a-birthday-or-a-party ideas.

The only person I never seem to bump into is Simon – though that must mean something.

I'm a little bit relieved (though I wouldn't even tell Mycroft Christie that).

But I can't avoid him when Venables calls a grand PAG meeting in the auditorium, with compulsory attendance for all.

"Brilliant, brilliant, come in, do!" he yelps, hair flapping as he beckons us in from the cold.

The auditorium has got its festive party mojo going too. All the tiered seats have been pulled out and pushed forward, taking over what was empty rehearsal space and throwing all attention towards the stage, where giant plywood stiletto heels and cocktail glasses are stacking up. There are inflatable flamingos dangling from the lighting rig. Tucked away in the wings are rows of metal wardrobe frames, where I can see some of the finished costumes hanging up: silver flashes mixing with ribbons and epaulettes.

We climb into the weirdly bouncy seats, precariously raised up above the stage, and I somehow end up sitting between Henry and Simon. Henry whispers rapidly into my ear about his brilliant idea for an Unparty for Dai's Unbirthday, while Simon says nothing: just stares mistily into the distance through his hair in a way he probably thinks is enigmatic and sort of sexy.

I can see Dai watching me keenly, an "I thought so" look on his face.

OPE.

OO.

He thinks it's Simon too.

I try to catch Ludo's eye but she seems to be ducking mine suddenly.

I don't want to look at Fili, a few rows below; it's all too awkward.

"So, guys, guys, thank you for coming!" says Venables, skipping a bit with excitement. "Now, I know you've been working hard, I know you're all tired, so I thought it was time you had a little break, and a little treat."

There's a chorus of oohing. Apparently no one else is as worried as me about what Venables' idea of a treat might be.

"So this weekend we're going to fly away from the Goldfinch nest and see how the professionals do it. Not a musical version, no, but after Mr Prowse expressed a few, uh, *concerns*, Mrs Kemble is very keen to emphasize the educational aspect of this year's performance to your parents. So we'll be heading to the theatre to see *Twelfth Night*, the original William Shakespeare, no-help-from-me version. Brilliant, yeah?"

There's no oohing.

"And of course, it'll be a late night, so we'll be staying over in Stratford, and coming back by coach the next day."

Now there's oohing. And shrieking, and even, from one corner, a round of applause.

Not from me though.

I should be thrilled. This won't be just like any other school trip I've been on before. This time I'll have someone to share a seat with on the coach instead of having to sit next to Timo, someone to keep my seat in the theatre, someone to sneak out of bed for once the teachers have gone to sleep, just like a real Finch; like a real girl, with a real boyfriend. I'll be on the trip with my Mysterious E. I just wish he wasn't Simon, that's all.

Venables is still beaming and waving his arms in front of us, flapping some papers to get us to quiet down.

"That's not all, folks, there's more good news! Now, I know everyone in this room is super-talented in their own way, and you know I'm proud of you all, yeah? But a lot of your work goes on behind the scenes, and on the big night it's all about the performers, so I'm totally thrilled to have a chance to big up one of the real stars of the show. You've all seen our amazing costumes, yeah?"

There are murmurs of approval in the crowd, as Venables flings an arm to the wardrobe racks at the edge of the stage. He grabs a curled pile of papers and waves them over his head. Teddy's designs. I start to feel a bit sick.

"Well, I was so impressed with the work that went into these, I showed them to Mr Bowser in the art department, and *he* was so impressed that he's entered the artist into the Independent Schools National Arts Prize. Heidi? Heidi, give us a wave, yeah? Brilliant."

Henry grabs my arm and waggles it about, as people clap and cheer.

UM.

UR.

EEK.

There's a blur of people moving round me, climbing over the rows of seats, telling me how amazing I am. Even Etienne Gracey leans over to give me a quick pat on the back.

I manage to get on to my feet and start edging my way along the row, mumbling apologies as I push past the slow-moving people on the steps down to ground level. I have to tell Venables. It'll be awful and horrible and everyone will hate me, but I can't let them put me up for some daft prize. I have to tell the truth.

I let the crowd sweep me out through the doors into the foyer, then duck through Music Room 1, find the backstage steps and hurry up into the wings. Venables is at the front of the stage, kneeling down and muttering something about spotlights to Oliver Bass.

I hesitate, waiting for him to stand, then I force my feet, one in front of the other, to move me forward, out on to the stage. It feels strange, seeing the seats all rising up out of the dark out there, all facing my way.

My feet keep on stepping, but someone has my arm and is pulling me back. Dai. Dai, with a face like thunder.

"I don't know what you think you're doing, Ryder, but you can knock it off right now, yeah?"

I blink. Does Dai know that Teddy drew the pictures? Does Dai *care* that Teddy drew the pictures?

"You two might think you're being dead clever," he says, yanking me into the wings, behind the guilt-inducing racks of costumes. "But I'm not blind. I do see things. Especially if you carry on with it right under my nose."

Not the pictures then. Simon. He's angry with me about Simon. I think.

"Why do you care?" I stutter, looking round and hoping no one else is listening. I'm having a fight over a boyfriend I don't even want. Does *Dai* want to go out with Simon then?

Dai goes from looking furious to looking like a kicked puppy in the blink of an eye. His big shoulders drop. I think for an awful moment that he might actually cry.

"I really like him, Heidi. He's the first person I've ever really liked, who really liked me back. At least, I thought he did. But then I started watching you, because . . . well, never mind why. I just knew you were looking for someone else after you'd broken up with Ed, and then suddenly you two were sneaking off together to talk, and he started being all secretive, and—"

"Wait. You think . . . me and *Henry*. . .?"

And I thought I was the hopeless detective around here.

"Well, why else would you go off for your secret get-togethers?"

My mouth opens but then I close it again. I can't spoil Henry's birthday plans, not now. Especially not now.

Dai doesn't wait to hear it anyway, just sticks up his chin and stomps off down the backstage steps, pushing Ludo out of his way as he goes.

She stares after him, hesitating at the bottom of the stairs, then hurries up them to me.

"OH MY GOD, what is HIS problem?"

I just shake my head. Explaining is a bit beyond me right now.

Ludo hovers, gazing up at the lighting rig above, the invisible audience beyond, her eyes shiny. Her painted fingers walk along the row of hanging costumes, toying with the dangling ribbons.

"OK, like, this is probably a totally weird question," she says, looking strangely shy. "But, like, I just wanted to check that it would be OK with you first, because . . . well . . . you've got a new boyfriend now, right?"

"Um . . . kind of?"

"I totally thought so. Which is, like, yay Heidi! So, you know, you won't be getting back together with Ed?"

The sick feeling comes back.

"Because if you aren't going out with him, then I thought maybe I might go out with him? Actually, we're sort of going out already. Or, you know, talking about it. Kind of?" She flips her glossy hair back and gives me a nervous little smile. "He's really sweet, isn't he?"

"Yeah," I mumble. "He's . . . um. . ."

"I'm so happy!" she says, wrapping her arms round my neck. "Because I totally wouldn't if it wasn't OK with you, and I would totally understand if it wasn't, because, you know, friends don't do that to each other. But if you're OK with it then everything's, like, totally perfect!"

And she goes pirouetting off down the steps, leaping over the last couple in full view of a loitering Peroxide Eric, with a look of gleeful don't-care upon her face.

Evasive manoeuvres, captain. Abort, abort! Engage the hyperdrive immediately.

I peer out from behind the sleeve of Viola's pink jacket, looking for an escape route. The wings on the opposite end of the stage are blocked up with giant sparkly shoes and lipsticks. Venables is still out front, showing off Teddy's sketches, now joined by a little crowd: Etienne, and The Illyrians and . . . the Mothership. I turn to head back through the music room, but brushing past Eric and stalking determinedly up the steps is Fili.

I retreat backwards, into the scratchy silvery safety of the Niteclubbers' clothes rail, enveloping me like some kind of spandex route to Narnia. I can't do this now. I'll fix it later. I promise I'll come back and sort it all out, when my head isn't spinning around with all the craziness of Dai and Henry, and Ludo and Ed, and Simon.

Fili's pointy black boots appear beneath the gold sequinned skirt that Yuliya will be wearing. They stop, exactly where I'm hiding: just centimètres away.

I bite my lip, waiting for her to sweep back the sparkles and ask me what the hell I'm doing crawling around on my knees. But instead another pair of boots join hers: scuffed, and much bigger, but just as pointy. And that makes me bite my lip even harder.

"Simon, *please*," I hear Fili say.

"I know. You told me to stop trying. I'm sorry."

"Don't be sorry. You haven't done anything to be sorry for, just don't—"

"I'll stop. I'll give up on us, I will, if that's really what you want. If you'll just tell me why."

A pause.

"Can't," she whispers, before one pair of boots patters away down the stairs, swiftly followed by the other.

I can, I think. But I won't. I won't need to now, anyway. Mysterious E isn't Simon. Mysterious E never could've been Simon.

I should be relieved, but I'm not sure it matters. I've messed everything up. Gingerbread Ed, and E.D. Hartley, and Fili: it's all gone too far, and I don't know how I can take it all back.

gingerbread_ed
Subject: goodbye

hey,
i'm going away on an exchange trip to peru where i hear they don't have the internet probably. so i guess i won't be around much because it is a very long exchange trip. sorry about everything.
ed

To: bloodwinetears@letterbox.com
From: gingerbread_ed@frogmail.com

Dear Fili,
I'm sorry but I think I have to stop writing to you. I can't really explain properly, and I really hope you know you have other people around you who would love to be able to talk with you like the old days. But with me and Heidi not being together and everything, now seems like the right time to call this a day.
Ed

To: gingerbread_ed@frogmail.com
From: bloodwinetears@letterbox.com

Dear Ed,
Your timing is better than mine. I'm late.
I think I'm pregnant.
Fili

Recipe for The End of the World

Ingredients:

No friends
No life
No hope

Method:

- It is too late
- There is no method
- Just stand back as everything falls apart

An attic. Ridiculous fictional detective Mycroft Christie is inexplicably present, talking to the unfortunately-not-imaginary Miss Heidi Ryder.

HEIDI: I don't know what to do.

MYCROFT CHRISTIE: Nonsense! There's always a Plan B.

HEIDI: Yes. And a Plan C, and a Plan D, and Plan Z, and all of them will be stupid, like making up people who don't exist, and handcuffs, and thinking I'm a detective when I'm too stupid to notice anything at all, and all of it is no use anyway because there's actual real proper difficult life stuff happening to actual real people. I don't need a Plan. I need to help my friend Fili. Go away, please?

MYCROFT CHRISTIE: I'm afraid I can't. I'm your subconscious mind's default response whenever faced with a crisis.

HEIDI: Can you *fix* the crisis?

MYCROFT CHRISTIE: I can defuse nuclear weapons with a fountain pen?

HEIDI: Nice. Can you help Fili?

MYCROFT CHRISTIE: (smouldery eyebrow, seductive nostril-flare, manly-yet-vulnerable teardrop on brink of falling)

HEIDI: That's really helpful, thanks.

MYCROFT CHRISTIE: At least I'm here for you to talk to. After all, you aren't exactly blessed with potential alternatives. Betsy is somewhat preoccupied with moving, thanks to your failure to rescue the Little Leaf. The Mothership would have to involve the school, and her parents too: perhaps not the most diplomatic choice? And as for friends. . . Young Dai seems to be under the impression you're rather devious: I doubt he'll want to listen. Dear Ludo is unfortunately besotted with . . . well, *you*, not that she knows that: more than a little awkward. Then there's Simon, who doesn't love you after all: how tragical, to be disappointed about someone you never even wanted. Though of course you couldn't tell him anyway – even if he were the potential father, which, after all, is hardly certain. . . No, definitely best not to tell Ludo. . .

HEIDI: It's not them I want to talk to anyway. It's Fili.

MYCROFT CHRISTIE: But Miss Heidi Ryder knows nothing. Fili didn't choose to tell her: she told dear, kind, sensitive Ed.

HEIDI: It doesn't matter. If people find out about Ed, it doesn't matter, not now. I don't care.

MYCROFT CHRISTIE: Don't you think Fili might care? Don't you think Fili might be even more hurt, to learn the one person she thought she could trust was nothing but cinnamon and dust?

HEIDI: So what am I supposed to do?
MYCROFT CHRISTIE: Don't ask me. I don't exist.

To: bloodwinetears@letterbox.com
From: gingerbread_ed@frogmail.com

dear fili,
i don't know what to do. do you want me to tell someone about this?
do you want me to help?
ed

To: bloodwinetears@letterbox.com
From: gingerbread_ed@frogmail.com

dear fili,
tell me what to do?
ed

To: bloodwinetears@letterbox.com
From: gingerbread_ed@frogmail.com

dear fili,
i wish you'd talk to me.
ed

To: heidi.ryder@goldfinch.ac.uk
From: arealboy@letterbox.com

Dearest Heidi,
Patient as I am, I find myself feeling dreadfully neglected of late, and

contrary to popular song we do not have all the time in the world.

Might I beg for a fragment of your kind attention? Or should I fear your attentions are truly swayed in the direction of another?

Rest assured, you continue to have my

love & affection,

E

To: arealboy@letterbox.com
From: heidi.ryder@goldfinch.ac.uk

Dear E,

Look, now is really not a good time for all this stupid messing about pretending to talk funny, all right? Some of us have more Important things to worry about.

Just forget about me, please? Because, whoever you are, I'm really not worth it and I totally don't have time for this.

Heidi

To: heidi.ryder@goldfinch.ac.uk
From: arealboy@letterbox.com

Dearest Heidi,

How terribly intriguing you are determined to be. But please, leave the noble sacrifices to the gentleman of the party? I can't play my part if you steal all my best lines, after all.

As ever, I am at your service.

love & affection,

E

(PS – seriously, you ok? I can't ever tell when you're kidding.)

I almost crack on the way up the hill the next morning, and cut into the Mothership droning on about Mrs Kemble's plan to bulldoze the tennis courts to tell her that the world is, you know, ending. But I can't get the words out. It wouldn't be fair, anyway. That's up to Fili to decide, after I've given her a hug, and told her it'll all be all right somehow. Even though it might not be.

I get evils from Dai and confusion from Henry, odd hurt whispers about Peru from Ludo, nervous looks from Simon and Eric, who are probably wondering why I'm staring. I get nothing from Fili, because she's not in French, or History, or the potato queue at lunchtime. I can't really blame her for hiding out. A bit of me wants to hide out, too: just flop in front of the big plasma in the common room, and slip into a world where hitting ninjas could make all the problems vanish.

But I have to track her down, and her bedroom is the obvious place. I leave the dining hall potatoless, and head for the Manor, hoping it'll be someone else in the cubbyhole I can sneak past more easily, but Dad Man's on the day shift.

He flaps his hand at me sternly, but I shout something about being sent to check on an ill student over my shoulder as I bolt up the stairs. It's sort of true, after all.

She's not there, though. Just Yuliya, who flaps a limp arm vaguely towards the front gardens.

I scoot back down the stairs.

"Sorry, I know, won't happen again!" I call breathlessly to Dad Man, running down the corridor (head firmly turned away from the Student of the Year board, as if not looking at it will make it disappear) and out on to the front steps.

Fili's there. A little black cloud, sitting on the steps.

It makes it a bit hard to hug her.

Maybe hugging isn't appropriate, anyway?

That was the only bit I planned though. I'd imagined after that it would all just kind of flow, and I'd know what to say. But now she's blinking up at me, looking a little surprised, and suddenly I wish I was safe behind my keyboard, behind Ed, who seems to know how to do this sort of thing much better than me.

"Are you all right?" I say.

She shrugs.

"Only . . . well, Ed told me that maybe you . . . weren't. . . All right, I mean."

She blinks and laces her fingers together on her knees.

"Ed told you that?" she says very quietly.

"Um. Yeah. Because we still talk, sometimes. A bit. I mean, not very often, but. . ." I get very interested in the end of my left plait suddenly. "Anyway, he said I should talk to you, so. . ."

I look back to Fili. She's looking up at me, straight at me, her eyes big and shiny with tears.

I've ruined it. I knew I would. Ed was the one person she trusted enough to tell, and now I've made her think he's broken that trust.

The bell goes inside, for afternoon lessons.

"You'd better go," says Fili dully, looking away down the drive.

I feel my insides go all shrivelled as I hurry back up the steps.

Fili doesn't come to classes again the next day. No one else seems to notice: they're all too busy talking about the *Twelfth Night* trip: what to wear, where to shop beforehand, who's got a fake ID good enough for the pub. All except Simon, who just drifts around looking lost and sad, reminding me of the reasons why he should: ones he doesn't even know.

To: bloodwinetears@letterbox.com
From: gingerbread_ed@frogmail.com

dear fili,
i hope you're ok. i'm sorry if me telling heidi wasn't the right thing to
do. i just want to help. tell me what i can do to help?
ed

I don't expect her to answer. I don't expect her ever to talk to either
of us again. Gingerbread Ed, with his broken-off arm sitting
crumbily at his feet, really isn't worth talking to. But I suppose when
you're desperate and alone, you take what you can get.

To: gingerbread_ed@frogmail.com
From: bloodwinetears@letterbox.com

Dear Ed,
Don't worry about me. Heidi won't have to worry about me either, very soon.
I'm going to fly away. Escape the nest, the very next time they open the cage.
Fili

To: bloodwinetears@letterbox.com
From: gingerbread_ed@frogmail.com

dear fili,
do you mean you're running away? please don't. i really think you
should talk to someone before you do anything like that. or just don't
do it at all? please?
ed

fili,

please let me help you?

ed

"If you don't want to go on the theatre trip, babes, you don't have to."

The Mothership stares anxiously at my untouched plate of mashed-up butternut squash and pumpkin seeds, which I probably wouldn't have wanted even if it didn't feel like I have a canoe in my throat.

But I shake my head and tell her I want to go. Yuliya's been telling people Fili's got a cold, but I bet she'll be well enough to come on the coach. I'm just scared she's not planning to come back.

Which is how I end up on my way to watch a comedy about cross-dressing shipwrecked twins when reality is rollercoastering its way off a cliff: not in space, not in a pirate ship, not with any monkeys or explosions or leather trousers. Just an ordinary cliff, with ordinarily hard, pointy rocks at the bottom.

I try to sit next to Fili on the coach but Ludo spotwelds herself to my elbow and talks Ed all the way there.

I try to snag a shared room with her in the hostel they've booked for the overnight stay but Prowse has allocated the rooms, and she's down the other end of the hall.

I try to sit next to her in the theatre but Henry grabs my arm and forces me to sit between him and Dai, to Dai's obvious irritation. I shoot out of my seat at the interval, to see if I can sit next to her for the rest of the play.

But she's not in the bar: not in the toilets, not in the theatre at all.

I can hear Venables yelling after me as I sprint down the stairs, but I'm not stopping for him or anyone. I run back the five-minute walk back to the hostel, heart pounding. We're in funny little dorms in an annexe round the back of a hotel, the kind that knows what teenagers smell like and doesn't want us to puke on the proper paying customers over their bacon and eggs in the morning. Girls on one floor, boys on the other, two bunks to a room. I hurry past the room I'm sharing with Ludo, past all the others, hoping I've remembered the number right, hoping I'm not too late.

Fili's at the other end of the hallway, sharing with Yuliya. Room number 13. An omen. Just has to be.

I hammer on the door.

Silence.

I hammer again, dropping my hands to rest on my knees, resting my head against the door to catch my breath. Then there's a click, and I'm falling forwards, knocking her back on to the lower bunk.

She's still here.

She's still here.

She looks cold and sort of angry. Fully dressed, eyelinered, boots on.

Her suitcase is on the floor by her feet, zipped up, waiting.

"Aren't you missing the play?" she says, quietly.

I get this spooky little flash of us together, in the dining hall, just after I first arrived when I was still terrified of everything and everyone and still hadn't figured out that you could say "no" to gravy. And most of all, I was terrified of Fili who had come to sit at my table, without saying anything at all. She just sat there eating a sandwich, watching me chase bits of carrot through the scummy brown lake on my plate without even slightly pretending she wasn't. Then Jo-Jo walked up like he was going to sit down too, and she gave him a look, the look, the Go Away look, and he did. She went back to looking at me, and somehow I wasn't getting the Go Away look: same eyes, same lack of words, but not the same at all.

I'm getting the Go Away look now.

It hurts but I've probably earned it.

Fili lifts a hand up, rests it on the top of her case, drums her fingers like she's waiting for me to leave. I nearly do. But that's not what I came here for.

"Look, just . . . don't run away, yeah? I mean, if you were thinking of it."

She rolls her eyes, unzips the suitcase and lets it fall open. It's empty.

"Oh. So . . . you're not running away then?"

She shakes her head slowly.

"Oh. Well, good. I thought you . . . I mean, Ed thought. . ."

She flips the suitcase lid down again and looks at me sadly.

OH.

OH.

Something in my head clicks into place.

"You know, don't you?" I say, my voice coming out all thick. "About Ed. I mean, you know he's. . ." I swallow. It feels so odd, saying it out loud. "He's not real. He never was real. I just . . . made him up."

Fili nods, just once.

I flop down on the bunkbed, next to her. "I always did think he was kind of obvious. Poetic boy with motorbike who no one can ever meet, who happens to fall madly in love with me? I didn't really expect anyone to believe in him."

"You just put him on the Internet by accident. And then wrote all those messages. By accident."

I feel my toes knotting together, and hang my head. It's probably a good thing we're sitting side by side. Makes it easier not to see her face.

"It just kind of got out of hand, honest. Dai and Ludo started talking to him, and it seemed like it couldn't hurt anyone, you know?"

"It hurt me," she says.

OW.

"Think I was jealous," she says with a tiny sad smile.

"But I was jealous of you! You had Simon, and you seemed like you were so happy, and always together. And you never talked to Ed like the others did – though I suppose I get why, now. I thought you didn't like me any more."

"I thought the same thing about you," she says slowly. "I wanted to talk to you. Not Ed-you, Heidi-you. I wanted to tell you how confused I was. How awful I felt, about. . ."

I look up as she cuts herself off and shakes her head.

"I don't know why I'm angry with you," she sighs. "It's me who screwed up. Messed everything up for Ludo, spoilt everything with Simon. I . . . I slept with Eric."

I squirm on the bed. "I know. I mean, I figured it out. Eventually."

"I've wondered if you knew for ages," she says, sounding almost relieved. "The way you kept staring at him; like you knew something wasn't right."

I squirm a bit more.

She sighs and twines her fingers in the tassles of her scarf, looking impossibly sad.

"You want to know what hurt me the most, though?" she says, not looking up.

I look at my feet. I don't even know what the worst of it is; there are way too many contenders for the prize.

"The worst of it is . . . you actually believed all that emo crap I wrote."

HUH?

A wan smile tugs at her lips.

"I don't send complete strangers emails about my rainbows of despair, Heidi. 'The garden of love is a thorny threshold'? I'm offended. When I do pain, I do it better than that. I kept expecting you to call me on it, but, well, apparently that's what I am to you. The sad clown, with tears on her face."

"I didn't draw that," I blurt out.

She raises an eyebrow. Drops it again. Comes up with a totally unexpected rueful laugh. I haven't seen her do that in. . . I'm not sure I've ever seen her do that.

"We really are the cock-up twins," she sighs, all the coldness gone from her voice now.

"So – you were just messing around? All that stuff about being unhappy, that was just a joke? To punish me?" I put my hand up to my mouth, trying to cover up my little gasp. "Did you make up being *pregnant*?"

Her face alters, like it's trying to close itself up.

"Not exactly. I thought. . ." She puts a hand on her tummy and frowns. "I didn't make up being frightened. Needing a friend. And by the time I knew for certain that I wasn't. . ."

"I'd already screwed it up."

I've been the worst friend imaginable. I thought I must be lonely to have to make up a Gingerbread Ed, but Fili *only* had him to talk to. No Ludo because of Eric; no Betsy, no Mycroft Christie, not even a Mothership.

"I'm so sorry, Fili."

She shrugs. "Team effort. Don't think either of us was thinking all that straight. I do get why you kept Ed around, you know. It was fun for a while, pretending to be someone else, talking up all my problems, waiting for it to sound bad enough for you – the real you – to step in. Only you wouldn't do it. You kept my secret, *all* my secrets, to stop anyone from finding out yours. All to protect a boy who doesn't exist."

She stops and sighs, as if using up an entire month's word quota in one go has worn her out a bit. As if she might change her mind, and go back to hating me.

There are totally other reasons, I want to say: other really good reasons, like me thinking Ed could help her more than useless thoughtless Heidi, and all those times I wanted to say something, and how I thought she'd never forgive me if I did tell, and how much I *missed* her, but then the Eric thing got so confusing, and Simon, and Mysterious E, and. . .

WOE.

UH.

I can hardly get the words out.

"Fili . . . are *you* E? Are you A Real Boy?"

She blinks at me. "No idea what you're talking about. Things are definitely back to normal."

They aren't, I know, not really. It'll take a little while for that. But she smiles, and I remember what I've been trying to do forever, and give her a hug. She hugs me back. It's the best feeling in the world.

"You can tell the others," I say, kicking at the ugly pink carpet. "Or I'll tell them. About Ed, I mean. If you want. They'll never speak to me again, probably, but I kind of deserve that."

Fili frowns. "Are you going to tell Ludo about Eric and me?"

"No," I say without hesitating. "They're over now. They were already over. She's better off without him anyway. It'd only hurt her feelings."

"So how about you keep my secret, I'll keep yours?"

Can it be that easy? Is this a test?

"I'll delete him completely," I say in a rush. "I won't write any more messages from Ed, to anyone. Just total and complete honesty from now on, I promise."

She nods, then chews on her lip.

"I suppose I owe that to Simon too," she sighs. "I should tell him about Eric, at least."

"He'll forgive you."

She looks surprised by how quickly I answer.

"Fili, he'd forgive you if you told him you killed puppies for a hobby. And then made earrings out of their teeth. You two are just kind of meant to happen."

She blinks, and allows a small, hopeful smile to creep back into the corner of her mouth.

"Yeah, maybe," she admits. "What about you though? What was that about a Real Boy?"

I blush and fiddle with my hair, and start to explain.

Heidi and Fili, hanging out and talking about boys, like best friends do.

Recipe for a Brand New Heidi

Ingredients:

An old, slightly worn Heidi
Friends
Honesty
The musical stylings of Kajagoogoo

Method:

- Take care to remove all traces of gingerbread, detectives, and boys (imaginary or otherwise) from your Heidi
- Soak her in tea and company for two weeks
- Unwrap her like a Christmas present

A dimly lit penthouse, which looks uncannily like a small, slightly untidy attic bedroom belonging to a fifteen-year-old girl. Mycroft Christie, time-travelling private investigator, is sulking, while Miss Heidi Ryder stares him down.

MYCROFT CHRISTIE: This is absolutely—
HEIDI: (holding up a finger sharply) Oi!
MYCROFT CHRISTIE: But I'm merely—
HEIDI: Final warning!
MYCROFT CHRISTIE: My dear girl, this is quite— I say, why am I walking into the wardrobe? And closing the door? And putting this pair of socks into my mouth?

HEIDI: I'm sure a detective genius like you will figure it out.
MYCROFT CHRISTIE: *Mmffwwwwhhfff.*
HEIDI: Couldn't have put it better myself.

"I knew there was a reason I was single," sighs Betsy, perching on one of the only chairs left in the strangely naked-looking Little Leaf.

"Trust me, I'm staying that way," I tell her, dunking my chocolate chip cookie a bit fiercely into my tea. "No more boy action for Heidi. Not that I've had any boy action. But if any comes my way, I'm sending it right back to the manufacturer."

"Oh, it's going to come your way, honey. You're quite the magnet. Straight girls, gay guys. . ."

"Have I mentioned lately how much I'm *not* going to miss you? Anyway, it was *Ed* who attracted Ludo, which is completely not the same thing. And I only attracted Henry inside Dai's crazy brain – which is all sorted out now, thank you."

"What about your mystery guy?"

"Mysterious E? Out of the picture."

"You figured out who that was, then?" yawns Teddy, shunting cardboard boxes across the floor with his foot.

"Nope. But I don't care. *No more boy action for Heidi.*" I tink my spoon against my mug with each word, just to drill it in.

Teddy blinks, gives me a slightly fearful look (which is probably fair enough; he doesn't really need to know about my boy action) and escapes out of the door with his boxes.

"It's probably for the best, hon. I mean, don't take this the wrong way, but he does kind of fit your pattern."

"My pattern? I have a pattern?"

Betsy dips her chin so she can peer at me over the top of some invisible glasses.

"OK, let's run through the selection of boys that seem to have been taking up all your energy lately. First up: Ed. Charming and all, but just a little bit on the imaginary side. Then we have the Mysterious E contenders, right? Which would be. . ."

"Eric."

"Dating one of your best friends."

Dating two, it turns out, though I'm pretty sure that's not going to help my case exactly.

"Then Simon."

"Dating another one of your best friends."

Also dating someone else, though I'm pretty sure there wasn't an overlap.

"Then Henry. Though *I* never thought that! All in Dai's hyperactive imagination."

"But he is. . .?"

"Dating one of *my* best friends." It still feels a little odd saying "best friends" like that. A week ago I was pretty sure I wouldn't have any. But you can fit a lot of apologizing and "can we just forget that ever happened" into a week.

I sulk into my tea, feeling guilty again.

"Yep, OK, I get it. I'm a big shameless boy-stealing ho. In my imagination, at least."

Betsy takes the mug away so I can't lurk behind it any more.

"No, honeypie, that's not it. The pattern's not that they're people your friends are dating. The pattern is that they're unavailable. Which makes them . . . safe. Like your gingerbread man. A boy can't hurt you if you made him up. And he can't break your heart if you'll never, ever get to date him."

"But that doesn't make him *safe*. That makes him . . . sucktastic. Not to mention a buttload of work. I've done the imaginary boyfriend thing; seriously, that is not a relaxing gig. I mean, not

194

that it matters now anyway, but Mysterious E's not the same deal at all."

"Really? So what is it you like about him? His taste in music? The colour of his eyes? His laugh, his walk, that cute little thing he does when no one's looking? Or do you like that he doesn't have any of those things, so you can make them up yourself?"

I take my mug back and frown into it.

"You can't control everything, hon," she says.

To: arealboy@letterbox.com
From: heidi.ryder@goldfinch.ac.uk

Dearest E,
Apparently I only ever liked you because you're a figment of my imagination. Or something. So this is goodbye.
H

To: heidi.ryder@goldfinch.ac.uk
From: arealboy@letterbox.com

Dearest Heidi,
How unfortunate: I was rather looking forward to my grand unveiling. I thought a certain forthcoming end-of-term event might be a suitably grand occasion?
Wouldn't you like me to prove my non-figmentary nature once and for all?
love & affection,
E

To: arealboy@letterbox.com
From: heidi.ryder@goldfinch.ac.uk

Dearest E,
No!
H

To: heidi.ryder@goldfinch.ac.uk
From: arealboy@letterbox.com

Dearest Heidi,
I'm not at all sure I'll be able to carry out your wishes on this subject,
my dear. We figments are rather stubborn that way.
You could always prove your utter disinterest by failing to reply?
love & affection,
E

To: arealboy@letterbox.com
From: heidi.ryder@goldfinch.ac.uk

Dearest E,
Honestly, I'm really not going out with people at the moment, so you
really shouldn't bother trying all this stuff.
H

To: heidi.ryder@goldfinch.ac.uk
From: arealboy@letterbox.com

Dearest Heidi,
Thank you. :)
love & affection,
E

The Finch is winding down for the end of term. The teachers have given up pretending to actually teach us anything, and lessons are now just finishing off bits of coursework, or falling asleep in the corner because you already have. The kitchen staff are all humming Christmas carols with a little 80s twist, thanks to the daily PAG rehearsals. I've even handed in a Poem on an Autumn Leaf to Prowse's satisfaction.

It's not all relaxation for me though. As part of my newly reformed truth-telling mission (Ludo quietly excluded, so I don't have to break her heart), I've confessed to Venables that I wasn't the one who drew the costume designs. Cue my first ever personal audience with Mrs Kemble, who is inconveniently not the Demon Headmistress after all (glowy red eyes, little horns hiding under her perm, mockable pointy tail) but the sort of person who says awkward things about me letting down my mum and dad, which aren't very mockable at all. The Mothership and Dad Man have tried quite hard to blame the negative influence of Finches, but I'm trying to cure them of that. I feel so guilty about this whole term, it's actually kind of a relief to be properly in trouble.

Plus my punishment is pretty entertaining. I'm on litter-picking duty every break-time as penance. I get to walk around the gardens dressed like a plasticated beekeeper, with a big prongy thing and a binbag – which happens to be the ideal outfit for Dai's birthday.

I do hesitate before heading over to the Lake common room, wondering if I really will be welcome. Henry ended up having to tell Dai he was planning a party, which ruined the secret *and* started a whole new fight about Dai's traumatic birthday history, and they almost broke up for reasons that weren't me.

But I'm curious to know how an Unbirthday Unparty works, beyond the invitation's demand to "Dress Unfestively". And Henry doesn't disappoint.

The common room has been Unimpressively Undecorated. There are popped balloons in multiple colours, flat limp blobs dangling pathetically off string. There's a banner strung up along the wall above the TV (playing *Brazil* on mute), with the words "Happy Birthday" masked out in black paint. On the coffee table sit jelly moulds shaped like rabbits, all empty: a silver-foil square of card has been speared with a single birthday candle, as if the cake in between the two suddenly vanished. And presiding over all is Henry, dressed in black, wearing a cone-shaped party hat (painted black, right down to the streamers), swaying gently to some epically miserable cello music.

I've never been to a funeral but I'm guessing this is pretty close. It's horrible. It's kind of tasteless. Dai's going to love it.

We do the obligatory hiding-behind-the-sofa-SURPRISE! bit. Dai does the obligatory I've-no-idea-you're-behind-the-sofa-I'M-SURPRISED! bit in return. Most of the Lower School PAG crowd turn up, all making the effort, suitably dressed down. It's as if, just for Dai, half the school's gone Novelty Goth – except for Scheherezade, who sticks out in her sparkly gold dress like tinsel in spring, and Fili, who has done her best to break with form, and is wearing a bright pink scarf of Ludo's on top of the usual uniform.

And then there's me, in my billowy plastic boiler suit, which turns out to be a bit sweaty when worn indoors.

"You've excelled yourself," says Dai, grabbing the prongy thing and trying to pick up a plastic cup (filled with only water, naturally) with its pincers.

"Truly, the least birthday partyish outfit I've ever witnessed," says Henry. "And waterproof too!" he adds, as Dai's prongy skills fail him.

I grin. "It's also sprayed with an antibacterial formula, which smells a bit like fish. Don't hug me."

They shrink back and then wander off to prong Scheherezade in the head, though Dai sneaks back later and gives me a hug anyway.

"Best birthday ever," he whispers, yanking on a plait.

I grin stupidly. I might nearly have messed it up. I might never be able to tell him the truth about Ed, but at least I helped Henry get this right.

My eyes search out Simon, and find him tucked in a corner, Fili's head bent close to his. She's told him about Eric already: looks like they might work it out after all.

Ludo flumps down next to me in an armchair, still somehow looking gorgeous, even wearing baggy pyjamas with her hair dragged into a scraggly top-knot. I still need to make all this up to her, somehow. I still see her pop up in UChat every now and then, looking for Ed, always hopeful that he might return from Peru.

I get a little ghost of an idea, of something that might do it. Just a gesture, like an early Christmas present. A really, really good, one-time-only, remember-this-for-ever Christmas present.

She leans over, tugging my plasticky arm.

"Oh my God, can you BELIEVE Dai thought you and Henry were, like, a thing?"

I look over to the two of them, mock-slow-dancing to the cellos in the middle of the room. Dai's ears are bright red, his cheeks glowing in pink patches, as if even he's just the tiniest bit self-conscious under all this attention. Henry's laughing, his hair sticking out under the elastic of the party hat, like he knows exactly what Dai's thinking; like he's proud of making it happen.

I can believe it, sort of. Because inside Dai's head he doesn't deserve all this: not wilted balloons, not invisible cakes, not a boyfriend at all, let alone this one.

And I think:

OH.

That's what I haven't got. I don't mean Henry. I don't even mean the slow dance with someone's hands at my hips, the silly whispered in-jokes, the eyelock as foreheads touch, then noses, then lips. Those I can invent: those I *have* invented. But I haven't got a boy who'll make me an Unparty while I'm not looking, because even though I say I don't want one I really do. I haven't got a boy who knows me better than I know myself. And I think I might sort of need one, because I don't think I know me at all.

Fili and Simon come to join us, perching together on the arm of the armchair, just as drawn into the slow dance of epic romance going on before us.

"They look so happy," Fili murmurs, slipping her feet under Ludo's legs to keep them warm.

"I know," Ludo sighs, hugging a cushion to her chest. "Oh my God, Heidi, LOOK at us? A load of hopeless single girls, staring at the unavailablest boys EVER. We're, like, SO pathetic."

"Wouldn't be so sure about that, you know," says Fili, that increasingly familiar smile quirking her lips.

Ludo's mouth opens wide as she looks over at Simon, and sees her pink scarf now looped around his neck. Then it opens even wider, as she realizes Fili is nodding my way.

"Nuh-uh!" I say, my plasticky arms making crinkly noises as I wave my hands. "Don't look at me. I'm not seeing anyone."

"Not *yet*."

"Oh my God, Heidi! Tell us EVERYTHING. And no being all secretive like last time! We need details. No, wait. Dai! Henry, stop snogging his face off and get over here!"

I shrink down in my antibacterial balloon, as Fili murmurs her way through an explanation of the adventures of Mysterious E (minus the extremely awkward bits). I keep expecting them to break out into total mockery at my pathetic attempts at romance, but instead they're just full of glee and questions.

"So is he a Finch? He must be a Finch."

"Has he given you any clues?"

"Is he hot?"

"Ludo, she doesn't even know his name, how's she supposed to know if he's hot?"

"She knows his name's E. If that's his real name."

"Whose name begins with an E?"

"Dude, it's probably a codename."

"What's the point of THAT? Doesn't he want her to know who he is?"

"That's all part of the game. You know, working it out?"

I glance up and catch Fili's eye, hoping I can show her how grateful I am. But she's glowing herself, at the easy, silly conversation, at being a part of it all, again, excited just as much as me. We've both missed this.

"Like detectives?"

"I suppose."

"Can we be detectives?" Ludo nudges me with a pointy elbow. "I bet we'd be really good detectives."

"We could have outfits."

"Disguises! We'll go undercover as . . . attentive students."

"We'll track him down for you, Ryder. Mysterious E isn't going to be Mysterious for much longer."

They're all grinning like idiots: Ludo, Dai, Henry, Fili, even Simon. It's the Leftover Squad, embarking on their very first investigation. And I don't even have to make it up.

Agent Ryder resumes her covert surveillance activity, which turns out to be much more fun when it's not quite so covert. After all, it doesn't really matter if we get caught. Dad Man can find Henry and Dai on the Manor stairs, dressed like ninjas, peering through the banisters to monitor the passers-by while I loiter as bait – and he just thinks we're being typically end-of-term weird. The Mothership can wonder why Fili and Ludo actually turn up to cross-country running for the first time all year – and dismiss their determination to run with the boys with the obvious explanation. And if Mysterious E happens to notice I'm being even more dorky than usual – well, he might just have to get used to that.

Trying to fit it all in around the last week of musical rehearsals doesn't get us very far with figuring out who my E could be. It's quite a relief to know I'm not the only rubbish detective around here. But I'm starting to get as nervous as they are, gearing up for the big performance. Giddy with anticipation, mildly terrified, sleepless at night, trying to picture how it'll go: whether I'll mess up my lines, fall over, faint the moment the spotlight hits me.

But I don't need to imagine it. I just have to wait.

To: arealboy@letterbox.com
From: heidi.ryder@goldfinch.ac.uk

Dearest E,
Will you really be at the musical? I mean, how will I know you're you?
H

Dearest Heidi,
A less determined soul might find your continuing bafflement
discouraging. Am I really so invisible?
As to the night itself, worry not. I imagine you'll find me easy enough
to notice.
Until the day, my enduring
love & affection,
E

And then it's here. The Big Day. The Season Finale. The Grand
Unveiling.

It's not all happiness. It's the end of term: tomorrow it'll be time
for awkward farewells in front of parents you'd forgotten these
people had, before all the shiny cars roll down the hill. The end of
the Little Leaf too. Saying goodbye to Betsy is going to be like
saying goodbye to cake itself. Promising to write and send pictures
to cake; being reassured that cake will call every now and then to
say hi; knowing that this will only remind you how you don't have
cake any more, and can never have cake again, when it's *cake*,
you know? Wondrous cake. (I'm not telling Betsy the cake
metaphor. It's possibly misinterpretable.)

I'm barred from helping out with the last-minute setting up in the
auditorium, thanks to the costuming embarrassment, so I try to
distract myself by heading into town for one last look at the crazy
walls, one last chance to smell the waft of tea and baking. I need
to ask Teddy for one last favour too, for Ludo's extra-special
Christmas present, if that isn't pushing my luck. Maybe I can even

get a little bit of the inevitable tearful hugging out of the way before I see them again tonight, up at the Finch. But the door's locked. The walls have already been painted over with grungy white. Even the furniture's gone.

I hope Mysterious E won't mind having a bit of a snotty girlfriend: I'm sniffly already.

He'll hold my hand though. Lend me a tissue. Sigh fondly at me, the way boyfriends do.

I head home, and waste the afternoon experimenting with the Mothership's waterproof mascara, until she's outside, honking the horn, and suddenly it's all beginning, for real.

The pillared Manor entrance is lit up with new spotlights, casting huge, distorted shadows across the stone as people pass the sparkling Christmas tree and head up the steps. We follow them through the corridor and down towards the lake, following the crowd and the slightly alarming scent of petrol. Venables' idea to light the way to the auditorium with tiny lanterns on boats, floating across the lake, seems to have been given to Jules Harper, resident pyro. Dad Man gives us a quick wave as he sprints past, fire extinguisher in hand.

The Mothership hurries over to mumble reassuring things to the gathered parental types in posh frocks, shooing them into the foyer. I follow their lead, like I'm just part of the audience.

The whole place looks adorable. I peep through the auditorium doors, to see the silver panels marking off the wings on either side (lined with familiar giant martini glasses), and the glittery "Orsino's!" sign suspended before the plush velvet curtains. A mirrorball revolves above the stage, sending faint hoops of light across the tiered seats, already filling up. But the foyer is decked out in a sparkly new party outfit too. The walls are draped with balloons and crêpe paper streamers; a machine pumps bubbles at the arriving audience, in strange irregular spurts, totally out of time with Huey Lewis thumping out of the crackly speaker system. It looks like a five-year-old's birthday party, only big.

Music Room 1 is the real transformation, though. There's already a crowd of people gathered beneath a glittery sign reading "The VERY Little Leaf", hung over the open doors. As they step aside, they reveal exactly that: the Little Leaf in miniature, like a doll's house version for real people, tucked in beside the usual shelves of glockenspiels and tom-toms. There's the same funny mix of mismatched cups and mugs, tables and chairs. Even the Sofa of Sex has been dragged up the hill for the occasion and plonked in the foyer. I can just see Betsy, pouring out tea, a pair of sparkly stars bouncing off springs on her hairband.

There's a chalkboard behind her, listing the menu: Rubik's Battenburg, Pop Rock Cakes, Electric Dreams and all the rest. I'm just being impressed by the highbrow Daily Wisdom – BECAUSE THOU ART VIRTUOUS, THERE SHALL BE NO MORE CAKES (*Twelfth Night, II.iii*) *apart from these ones!* – when I get tackled by a French maid and a giant rollerboy.

"HEIDI!"

I'm on the foyer carpet, with fishnets and skates and hairspray all over me. Ludo and Dai are apparently pleased to see me.

"Nice to see you too," I say, crawling back to my feet by tugging on Dai's kneepad.

He does an awkward little spin around me on his roller boots, then grabs me again, either in a hug or just to stop himself from rolling into Oliver Bass's mother.

No, it's a hug. Ludo joins in.

"Oh my God, Heidi, we worked it out!"

I detach myself from her arms, and try to guide us out of the path of incoming parents.

"You did?"

She nods wildly, though her backcombed mop of hair stays scarily still.

"We know who he is!" says Dai.

"We're, like, SO stupid!"

"Ridiculous, really. It's been staring us in the face."

"I mean, duh? E?"

I can't even get words out. I just stand there, waiting for them to spill.

"E, Ryder? E for *Etienne Gracey*?"

They both dance me around, making squeaky noises.

"Etienne Gracey! Isn't it, like, COMPLETELY amazing?"

I nod my head, feeling numb all over.

E.

E for Etienne.

Etienne, who broke up with Scheherezade at the Flick Henshall party.

Etienne, who's going to be wearing a grey leotard with neon-pink squiggly bits on it.

I imagine you'll find me easy enough to notice.

It's true. It really is him. Etienne Gracey, Upper School rock god: so cool he even has a band named after him. He really is him.

"Oh my God, Heidi! Like, SMILE?"

"Yeah, Ryder, seriously. It's Etienne Gracey, baby! How awesome is that?"

The crackling of Huey Lewis comes to a sudden stop, and Venables' voice mutters something incomprehensible through the static.

"Oh my God, we're totally supposed to be backstage!"

"Gotta fly. Don't tell me to break a leg or I'll have to kill you!" Dai skids off into the wall, till Ludo grabs him and starts to wheel him towards Music Room 3 and the backstage steps, both cackling gleefully as they wave and wish me luck.

Etienne Gracey.

I still feel numb. That's probably normal though. That's probably very romantic. I mean, I'm just surprised. It's just . . . not what I expected. I'm not disappointed, or anything like that. He's Etienne Gracey, after all. I mean, I've always thought he was a bit self-obsessed and kind of jerky, but E's not like that. And he plays guitar. Ed played guitar. I must like that kind of thing. Maybe that's where I got the idea. That's where this whole thing started, after all: me, sitting on the sofa at the McCartney Party, thinking Etienne liked me. It's all come full circle. It all fits together, perfectly, like on the TV.

It just doesn't quite feel like I thought it would, that's all.

I follow the last few people into the auditorium, hesitating in the doorway. The lights go dim, as the last few stragglers take their seats. I can just make out the Mothership waving at me, where she's saved me a place down near the front.

But then the stage lights go up and there's Henry in pink leggings and a candyfloss wig, yelling "If music be the food of love, then we're going to need some decibels, baby!" The stage is flooded with flashing lights and smoke. Finches appear: Fili the painted clown on a swing, Dai swirling around on his rollerskates, trying not to crush Ludo, as the speakers crackle out "Walk Like An Egyptian". The cloth backdrop falls to reveal Etienne and The Illyrians in their skintight neon-painted Tron bodysuits, miming with huge inflatable instruments.

I don't really want to be here, suddenly. I've been looking forward to this so much, and now I'm here, watching a musical about crazy space disco love, knowing someone who more-than-likes me is up on that stage, and it doesn't feel anything like I'd imagined.

I've messed up again.

I've got what I wanted, and now I don't want it at all.

Yuliya's onstage, towering over Henry in her own fluffy wig and stumbling her way through her lines slightly inaudibly. Scheherezade and Jambo arrive in a cloud of dry ice, military brass buttons shining, ribbons fluttering in the artificial breeze, to the strains of "Planet Earth". Scheh reappears as a boy, white stripe across her nose, to be flirted with by Henry (all watched by an increasingly intrigued Malcolm Malvolio, aka Dai, to the in-jokey glee of the audience). Fili continues to swing on her trapeze above them all, offering melancholy little snippets of David Bowie between scenes. Etienne and The Illyrians continue to rock out, as far as is possible when your guitars are inflatable and you're surrounded by people dressed as ice-cream cones and cocktail glasses, spinning around to "Club Tropicana".

It's no good. I can't pretend. I'm going to stick to gingerbread boys.

I fumble my way in the dark to the door handle, not daring to watch any more. I'm going to go and hide away in the Little Leaf for the last time. Drink tea. Eat cake. Maybe a gingerbread man (of the non-dusty variety), if they have any.

The auditorium door closes behind me with a whump, blocking out some of the noise, though the speakers still play a staticky, toned-down version, and there's a small TV screen showing the view from the very edge of the stage, courtesy of Venables' DV camera. It's cooler out here, at least. I creep over to the makeshift counter beneath the glittery sign, and find not Betsy but Teddy, propped on his elbows. He gives me one of his lazy smiles, then goes back to watching the show on the TV, chuckling at Ludo and Dai falling about.

"Your costumes look awesome," I say over the music.

Teddy shrugs. "Your ideas, remember?"

I shrug back. I've made sure his name's in the programme, but I still feel guilty. It's kind of cheeky of me to ask him for anything more –

but this one's not for me. I might be incapable of sorting out my own love life, but at least I can add a quick fizz to someone else's.

"Can I ask a little favour? It's kind of mental. And you can totally say no, if you think it's a horrible idea, only it would totally make her night, and I kind of feel like I owe her that, so. . ."

Teddy looks amused at me stumbling over my words, and twirls his finger, to speed me up.

"I just wondered if you wouldn't mind kissing Ludo." It sounds very mental, now I've said it, and his eyebrows have shot up into his hair. "I mean, not a huge full-on snogathon. Unless you wanted to. You could just give her a hug, even. Though, you know, if you think Safak would be upset, then obviously, forget I even mentioned it. . ."

"Safak?"

"Yeah. You know, Safak, your girlfriend?"

He smiles, ruffling his hair awkwardly. "We broke up. Quite a while ago. Round about the time you stopped working at the Little Leaf, actually."

OH.

Heidi, the great detective. Yeah, right.

"Sorry! I didn't know. I've been kind of not noticing what's right under my nose a lot lately."

The easy smile spreads across his face again. I shuffle my feet: guess I deserve being laughed at. Should be used to it from Teddy, anyway. I wait for him to make some snarky comment about how the glasses I clearly need are really going to set off my look, or whatever, but he's looking up. Not at the TV, or at the ceiling: looking up and tipping his head back a little, as if he wants me to look up above his head.

The Shakespearean Daily Wisdom has been wiped away. In its place, in Teddy's familiar twirly handwriting, it says

MUST I SPELL IT OUT?! *You have my love & affection, tEddy.*

OH.

MY.

GOD.

My hand flies to my mouth. I think some kind of squeaky noise gets out anyway.

"It's really that much of a surprise?" he says, his face falling.

I squeak again.

Yes?

"Yes, it is, it is, but . . . yes!"

He scrunches up one eye. "Could you say that again, because only dogs can hear you right now, and I'm sort of invested in the answer?"

I drop my hand away, and wrap my other around it to stop it shaking. Rest them both on the counter. Let one creep forward and take hold of one of his.

"Yes," I say, still all breathy and mouselike. "But . . . good surprise."

That smile comes along again. That Teddy smile that I've watched from afar: that I never, ever imagined could be for me.

"But . . . but . . . how? And when did you. . .? And . . . why did you. . .?"

"I've always thought you were pretty awesome, you know, on account of you actually being pretty awesome. Then suddenly you were inventing this boyfriend for yourself and I thought, hey, wait up, I'm feeling kind of jealous of this guy. Well, I think Safak was the one who figured that out actually. She thought it was kind of interesting you'd called him Ed. You know: Eddie . . . Teddy?"

I decide not to explain about E.D. Hartley; it can probably be saved for later.

"But why didn't you say anything?"

"Says the girl with the gingerbread boyfriend? I don't know, I thought the whole 'E' thing would be cute. Mom kept watching those DVDs of that show you like and . . . well, guess I was trying to cover my ass a little too. That Ed guy was kind of intimidating to live up to, you know?"

His hand tightens around mine, just slightly. Teddy's hand. Teddy's hand, holding my hand, like it doesn't want to let go.

"And I figured I was being pretty obvious – till you thought E was basically any unavailable, inappropriate guy in a forty-mile radius who wasn't me."

I bite my lip, feeling guilty again, though he's smiling.

There's a burst of static from the speakers. I glance over at the TV screen, and catch Etienne Gracey in his leotard, thwacking Brendan around the head with his deflating guitar. I decide not to mention him either. Though I don't think anything could ruin this moment: me, and him, my E, my perfect, not-imaginary, better-than-imaginary boy.

"Oh! But . . . you're going away!"

He sighs, dropping his head.

"Not for another week. And we'll be back to visit? But yeah, I know. I figured we'd work this out a little quicker. But you're kind of a master at email relationships already, right? If you think about it, we've been going out for weeks already, without even meeting. You think an ocean's going to get in our way?"

I shake my head, biting my lip to keep the squeakiness inside.

"Now, dearest Heidi, I have but one question to ask," he says, adopting a slightly wonky accent and attempting to look very serious, despite the on-screen vision of Honey Prentiss skipping across the stage dressed as a giant pink shoe. "And quit laughing. I worked pretty hard at learning how to talk like some stiff-assed Brit guy. So, dearest Heidi, my question?"

"Yes, Rupert?"

He gives me a stern look, then leans closer, a wicked twinkle in his eye.

"Still want me to kiss Ludo?" he whispers.

The speakers blare out "Take On Me", improbably on cue.

I shake my head.

I lean closer.

He doesn't taste like gingerbread.

Although I should probably kiss him again, just to make sure.

Recipe for Love

Ingredients:

Heidi
Teddy

Method:

- Just leave them to it

A dimly lit penthouse. Mycroft Christie, heroic detective, peers out of the wardrobe, slightly peeved to see every available surface in the apartment now covered with small, delicious-smelling gingerbread men. Glamorous Miss Heidi Ryder is a bit busy reading her emails to notice.

To: arealboy@letterbox.com
From: heidi.ryder@goldfinch.ac.uk

Dearest T,
Have you added more cinnamon? Extra yummy this week, anyway.
Though the postman is starting to think I'm involved in a thrilling
International import/export crime syndicate.
I & a,
H

To: heidi.ryder@goldfinch.ac.uk
From: arealboy@letterbox.com

Dearest Heidi,
Same here. Mom says "thanks for the teabags, now send another 5 million or so".
They weren't yummy before? I'm sulking here.
I & a,
T

To: arealboy@letterbox.com
From: heidi.ryder@goldfinch.ac.uk

Dearest T,
I'm sure the postman will just love me for that. Tell her she'll just have to visit?
Yumminess never in doubt, I promise. :)
I & a,
H

To: heidi.ryder@goldfinch.ac.uk
From: arealboy@letterbox.com

Dearest Heidi,
I don't know that they'd let her through customs, with that weird-guy shaped lump in her suitcase. Anyway, I hear the girl she might really want to visit spends all her time on the Internet, talking to some boy.
At least that's what she says. He sounds improbable to me.
I & a,
T

To: arealboy@letterbox.com
From: heidi.ryder@goldfinch.ac.uk

Dearest T,
Improbable boys are nice. But she likes real ones best of all.
l & a,
H

Recipe for Many Thank Yous (with cherries on the top)

All the tea in China to my Beloved Editors, Marion Lloyd and Rachel Griffiths, for rescuing Heidi, and seeing the things I couldn't: sincerely, I would be lost without you! Toasted teacakes to all you lovely folks at Scholastic (with an extra-buttery one to Alice Swan, for proposing big ginger beards: I'll put them somewhere one day, I promise). An especially jammy scone to Caroline Walsh, for trusting so wonderfully in my capacity to be not rubbish, despite all evidence to the contrary. Auntie Liz's shortbread to Jess, for hugely insightful brainy business: keep doing that, I need it! Slices of Battenberg all round to the lovely blog posse, here and there. Tall black Americano to Matt and his barista squad down at "the office": thank you for putting up with the weird mumbly person with the laptop at 6.59p.m. An endless supply of muffin tops to MG Harris, for your infallible chipperness, sense, and capacity to talk about Kerr Avon. Peanut butter brownies to Ruth Eastham, Josie Henley-Einion, Caroline Johnson and Sarah Mussi: onwards and upwards, ladies! And cinnamon-free gingerbread to B, for the socks (and other things too, but mostly the socks).

Finally, my enduring gratitude to Maggie Evans, for cheerleading for serafina, asking all the right questions, and introducing me to the Penguin. You were lovely, and we miss you.

Ta-da!

Don't miss Susie Day's hilarious

Susie Day

BIG WOO!

My not-so-secret teenage blog

My blog of lolarious brilliance
has escaped from the internets.
Into a book! BIG WOO!
Omg behold my interestingness.
But don't read it, tiny children.
It is full of rudey bits and lameassery,
AND SHOUTING IN CAPSLOCK
which is bad for you, obvs.

Serafina67